The Gore

Book Six of the Oz Chronicles

by

R.W. Ridley

Middlebury House Publishing

ISBN-10: 0979206774
ISBN-13: 978-0-9792067-7-1

Names, characters, places, and incidents are the products of the author's imagination or are used fictionally. Any resemblance to actual events, locales, or persons, living or dead, is entirely coincidental.

When the monster starts hiding from you, that's when you should be really scared.

- Unknown

Chapter One

"All I know how to do is kill things, Oz."

Light snowflakes swirled around Tyrone's head like falling ash. The words fell out of his mouth, but I don't know if he realized it. His eyes were locked on me, but I can't say he was looking at me. I don't think he was looking at anything. I think he could only see the images dancing around in his head. All the things he'd killed.

I could see them, too. The things I've killed. I knew how he felt. It's a strange thing having that kind of connection with someone: Killing things. Making things suffer. Removing things from this world. It didn't matter that this world was made up and twisted. It was still alive with creatures that were trying to do what we were trying to do, survive. And we killed a lot of them for it.

I didn't say any of this to Tyrone. I don't think I really had to. He knew the way things were. I had been there most of the way with him. We had seen and done the same things. He knew I was a killer, too. And some of the things we'd killed weren't just things. But calling them things made it easier to live with.

We sat on the hood of a mangled car on the outskirts of a small dead town that was no different than the hundreds of small dead towns we had passed through before. The others made their way through looted stores and restaurants searching for anything that could pass for food.

Tyrone spoke again. “I don’t know if that’s wrong or not.”

Chapter Two

We saw a man cut the hand off a corpse. He stuffed it in a bag he carried on his shoulder that was filled with other hands he had collected. He didn't explain himself. He just introduced himself as Floyd Templeton and asked if we had any supplies we could spare.

The strange thing is none of us asked why he had the bag full of hands. It wasn't out of place at all. It was how a world full of monsters and Storytellers worked. People, animals, mutants did brutal things to each other for no reason, or for reasons that didn't make sense.

He was a small man with thick salt and pepper hair and a pinched face. Other than his habit of slicing a knife through the skin, muscle, tendons and bones of the wrists of the dead, he wasn't a bad guy. In fact, he seemed unusually happy. If anything was out of place, it was his never-ending smile.

He was from Charleston. Like an idiot, I asked if he knew my uncle. He didn't. I knew he wouldn't. That would have been too crazy. He was a chef. Had his own restaurant. He demonstrated his skills by taking the blandest supplies we had and creating one of the tastiest meals any of us had enjoyed in a long time.

Floyd talked more than any human being I had ever known. He started laughing at one point, but none of us knew why. After almost throwing up, he explained. "Do you know how long it's been since I've seen this many people together? I mean live people. I come across dead people every day. Every thirty minutes in some parts of my travels. "

"How long you been alone?" Wes asked, wiping grease from Floyd's thrown-together gourmet meal from his chin.

Floyd thought about his question. "I'm not alone, exactly. There's some... a few others." He chuckled nervously. "Say, I don't know if I even know how many days have passed since this all started." For some reason, he didn't want to talk about the others in his group. "Any of you know what this is, by the way? I mean what happened to... everything?"

We all stared at each other. It was hard to explain without sounding insane. It didn't matter that the man we were trying to explain it to had a bag full of hands. None us of wanted to come off like lunatics.

He smiled. "I've heard all kinds of stories from strangers I've met. Heard it was a military experiment gone wrong. Heard it was the work of wizards and warlocks. Even heard the Devil had a hand in it.

"It ain't none of those things," Gordy said. "Well, I guess the wizards and warlocks come close."

Floyd waited for him to explain.

Instead, Gordy asked, "Where'd you learn to cook like this?"

Floyd hesitated and then said, "Growing up. My mom worked three jobs. She was never home to make us lunch or dinner or anything at all really. Had to learn how to cook so we wouldn't starve."

"Who's we?" Wes asked.

"Brothers and sisters. Two of each."

"Daddy?"

"Nope," Floyd said shoveling the last spoonful of food into his mouth.

Gordy licked his fork. "You learned this all on your own?"

"Some of it. The rest I learned in school."

"School? For cooking? They got those?"

Floyd laughed. "They do." He suddenly stopped laughing and added, "They did."

We all sat around the crackling fire and tried to shake the thought of how much things had changed.

"What do you mean about wizards and warlocks coming close?" Floyd asked, tossing his tin plate to the ground.

"He didn't mean anything," I said. "He's just talking."

Gordy looked at me confused and then said, "Yeah, I was just talking."

We could have told him what we knew. That the world was the way it was because of what I and others like me had done to kids like Stevie Dayton. That the monsters that destroyed our world were the monsters these kids created in comic books, and drawings and stories to help them escape how mean and unfair the real world was to them. That when Stevie died his monsters crawled out of the pages of his homemade comic book and tore the world apart just like he was torn apart. That other monsters followed. That this world was created by the Storytellers and ruled by the Destroyers. People like us were left behind to suffer for our part in the pain and misery we'd caused. We could have told him all that, but what was the point. The world had ended. How wasn't important.

Floyd leaned back and stretched out his legs. "However we got here, I can't say I hate it. Entirely anyway."

Tyrone glared at the man who collected hands and made gourmet meals out of nearly nothing like he wanted to punch him. "What do you know?"

Floyd pulled a pack of chewing gum out of his pocket and stuck a piece in his mouth. "Look at us. We're here out in the open, sitting around a fire, enjoying a crisp, cool night…"

"It's colder than hell," Wes said.

"Okay, it's cold," Floyd said, "but we don't have to be anywhere. We don't have jobs to get to. We don't have bills to pay. We don't have jury duty or stop lights or taxes or homeowners associations or any of that crap. It's just us. Five guys and two gorillas with nowhere to be and nothing we have to do. This is the real American dream!"

Tyrone practically growled. "I don't have Valerie. I don't have my grandfather. We don't have Kimball, Pepper, Roy…"

Floyd cut him off. "I get it. You lost people, but I hate to break it to you, kid, you were going to lose them anyway. You got something far more important out of all this. You got freedom. Can't always find that."

"That's enough," Wes said angrily.

"I didn't mean anything by it," Floyd said. "I just think it's better to see the good than it is to dwell on the bad."

Wes leaned forward. “That’s enough. I don’t want to hear no more about the good, bad, or ugly of it all. It just wears on me. Makes my brain hurt. It is what it is, and that’s all it is.”

“I get what Floyd’s saying,” I said. Everyone in my group shot me the evil eye. “There’s no way back so we might as well start thinking about it like that, seeing the good instead of the bad.”

Wes grimaced but didn’t say anything.

Gordy spoke up. “Wait. We can’t go back?”

Floyd smirked. “You think it’s possible? What’s gone is gone, kid. You can’t go back.”

Gordy was embarrassed by the stranger’s tone.

“Hey!” Wes barked. “Back off my boy!”

Floyd held up his hands. “I didn’t mean anything. I just think your son needs to hear the truth.”

“It don’t matter a squirt to me what you think,” Wes said. “And he ain’t my son.”

“Oh,” Floyd said. “I just thought…”

“That’s your problem. Those thoughts in your head got you all turned upside down on this thing. You know zero about how the world come to this. You know zero about what’s gone and what’s good and what’s bad. You just know zero, and that’s the truth you need to hear.”

Floyd shook his head and tried to hide a smile. “Okay, big man. Okay. I’m sorry I was out of line.”

“And for the record, I’d be honored all to hell to have any of these boys as my sons, but as it is they’re my friends. That’s the way of things here. Friends ain’t paired up by age. They’re paired up by circumstance and experiences. Hell, after what we’ve been through, they ain’t just my friends. They’re my brothers.”

Ajax let out a small garbled grunt.

"You too, old friend," Wes said. "And Ariabod."

"You see," Floyd said, "that's what I mean by good. You've got yourself a little band of brothers that I'm guessing you wouldn't have if the world hadn't gone to crap."

There was a moment of silence while we all thought over his point.

Gordy finally said, "You know, he's kind of right."

"He ain't right," Tyrone said standing. "Ain't nothing good ever happened here." He walked away.

"Sorry," Floyd said. "I should have let it go."

"Yeah, you should've," Wes said.

Floyd gathered up the dirty plates. "As punishment, I'll clean up."

Wes stood and took the dishes from him. "I'll get that. You best be on your way before too long. Don't want to get caught out in the dark."

"On my way?"

"Yeah, your people may get worried about you."

Floyd hesitated. "My people?"

"You ain't alone, are you?"

"Alone? No, I guess I should get back to my people." He reached down and picked up his bag of hands. "Thanks for your hospitality."

"Dude, you cooked," Gordy said. "We should be thanking you."

He nodded and headed up the path that led out of our campsite. We watched him turn a corner and disappear behind a thicket of trees.

"He doesn't have people," I said.

"What?" Gordy leaned back and tried to see if he could catch a glimpse of him through the trees.

"Probably not. That don't make him our problem," Wes said.

I stood and craned my neck trying to spot him moving through the woods. "Not good to be alone in this place."

"Not good to let strangers into your camp, either, but that didn't stop us."

"But he can cook," Gordy said. "We should let him join us if he's alone."

"No, we shouldn't," Wes said with a snarl. "We gotta be more careful about who we meet up with. We ain't got no idea about that fella. He could've been a serial killer back before all this happened. Or worse, a politician. I don't want to get stuck in a group with either one. Neither can be trusted."

"Am I missing something?" Gordy asked. "He's a cook. Did you not eat what he made us?"

"I did."

"And?"

"And it was tasty as all get out, but that don't make him trustworthy."

"Oz," Gordy said, "tell this joker we should let the cook in our group."

I gave up trying to see Floyd and sat back down. "Wes is right. We don't know anything about him."

Wes was a little surprised that I took his side.

Tyrone rejoined us. "We know enough about him."

"What do you mean?" I asked.

"He collects hands."

Wes, Gordy, and I hesitated and then started cracking up. Why none of us had brought it up until now, was a mystery. We had overlooked the creepiest thing about Floyd Templeton. He collected hands.

Chapter Three

This is how we spent our time, walking, searching for Lou, setting up camp, waiting for morning, and doing it all over again. It was the same, day in and day out.

I didn't sleep. Not for a long time. I couldn't. If I slept, I'd stop thinking about her. I didn't want to stop thinking about her. I suppose it was possible I'd dream about her, but I couldn't control my dreams. I was afraid of what my mind would cook up. I told myself she was alive. I'd even say it out loud in a whisper. Not loud enough for the others to hear. Just loud enough for it to be true. I thought if the words lived outside my body, they couldn't be denied. They had to be true.

We traveled hundreds of miles since she left us. Through the mountains, on once busy highways, through towns and neighborhoods, searching for her in every corner and shadow that we could find. There was no sign of her.

That changed once we reached the old fire tower on the Appalachian Trail in New Jersey. As soon as I saw it, I knew she had been there.

***

"Something happened here," Wes said standing at the base of the fire tower. He pointed to pools of frozen blood. "It wasn't pleasant, whatever it was."

Tyrone walked to the tree line and stared into the woods. "Carried out into the forest. Blood stains on almost every tree trunk." He stepped past the trees. "There's something…"

We waited for him to finish the sentence, but he never did.

"Something what?" Wes asked.

He turned to us. "I'm not sure if I'm seeing what I'm seeing."

The rest of us shared a curious look and then joined him.

He stepped back. "There past that tree broken in half."

I spotted the tree. "What about it?"

"Just past it, do you see what looks like a shelter?"

I worked to see through the snow covered branches until I found what he was talking about. "I see it."

"Keeping looking," he said.

I attempted to focus harder.

Gordy finally shouted, "I see it!"

"What?"

"A face."

Wes stooped down and peered over Gordy's shoulder in the direction he was pointing. He stepped back. "Holy…"

I still couldn't see what they were talking about, so I moved around the other side of them. "So it's a face? Maybe there's somebody out there…" I stopped when I finally saw it. It was a face, but it was upside down and there was no body attached to it that I could see. I made my way past the tree line.

"Hold on, now," Wes said. "We all agree it's a face, but by golly it ain't attached to nothing I can see, so I say we move on. We've all seen a head without a body before."

I hesitated before saying. "Lou was here, Wes."

He looked at the others and then said, "How in tarnation could you know something like that?"

"Because I know Lou. She was here. I can feel it. Before you tell me that's crazy, think about where we are and how we got here."

He thought about telling me I was crazy anyway, but he stopped himself. Instead, he signaled for me to go ahead. "Take the lead, young man. You always do."

I made my way through the icy snow-covered ground by grabbing hold of one tree after another until I reached the broken tree. I was out of breath just from trying to keep my footing. I could hear the others wheezing behind me. The gorillas stayed huddled together at the bottom of the fire tower.

"Good gravy," Wes said. "This air just plain stings the lungs. It's a good deal colder here than outside the woods."

"No kidding," Gordy said.

Tyrone moved around all of us and approached the face. "Well," he said, "It's not just a head. There's a body, too. Kind of."

I pushed myself away from the broken tree and stepped around it. The shelter was bigger than I'd thought. It was a collection of limbs woven together in a dome shape. Just inside the shelter was the head. And, Tyrone was right. There was a body. Kind of. It was a pile of body parts. The head was human, and the hands, but the rest of it was a hodgepodge of body parts from other animals.

"Oh man, that does not look good," Gordy said from behind me.

"Sure as crap don't," Wes said.

Tyrone almost laughed. "What? We've seen worse."

"Maybe," Wes said, "but that don't make it good."

Tyrone waved him off. "Something just threw out its table scraps."

I turned to Wes. His frown indicated he was horrified by what Tyrone had said and how he'd said it.

Gordy responded, "Ain't it a little too neat to be table scraps?"

I tried to see what he saw. Rotten flesh and jagged bones made up most of the pile. It was far from neat.

"You and me got a different notion of what neat is," Wes said. "That's just an ugly pile of meat and bones."

"But look at the way it's stacked," Gordy said.

I stepped up next to Tyrone with my eyes focused on the pile. Gordy was right. It was stacked neatly.

"Whoa," Gordy said falling back.

"What's got into you?" Wes asked, grabbing him before he fell to the ground.

Gordy's face was as white as the snow that surrounded us. "Was his... I mean the head... was its eyes open before?"

We examined the face. The eyes were open. They were pale, dead eyes. Something I was sure I would have noticed before.

"Course they were," Wes said.

"Yeah, had to be," Tyrone added.

"Why?" Gordy said. "Had to don't really go along with the way things work around here. That stupid thing opened its eyes..."

I motioned for him to be quiet. "If you didn't see them open, then they were already open."

"Says who?"

"Says me," I said. "We don't need to get all wound up about something that may not have happened."

He barked and jumped back.

"What is it now?" Wes asked.

"They blinked!" Gordy said. "I swear they blinked."

Tyrone rolled his eyes. "You're seeing things. I've been looking right at it."

"No, you turned away for a second. I saw you. That's when it blinked."

"If you saw me turn away, how did you see it blink?"

Gordy fumbled for an answer. "I just did. Alright."

Wes threw up his arms. "There you happy, Oz? You done drove Gordy out of his tiny mind. He's seeing eyes blink and heads turn and goodness knows what else. All because you had to come back here and see this pile of mess." He grabbed Gordy by the shoulder and pulled him back. "Let's get before you pee yourself or worse."

When they were in the clearing and out of earshot, I asked Tyrone if the eyes had opened.

He shrugged. "Who knows?" He approached the pile. "You know what our problem is?"

"I could name a few."

"We don't have enough fun."

"Fun?"

He raised up on his toes and reached for the head.

"What are you doing?"

"Having a little fun." He grabbed the hair and tugged on it.

"Stop," I said backing away.

"C'mon. I'm just going to play a joke on Gordy."

"With the head?"

"You think he freaked out when he thought the eyes blinked. Wait until he finds it in his sleeping bag tonight." He jerked as hard as he could and the head moved slightly.

"Leave it, Tyrone."

He looked at me. "Oz, when is the last time I had some fun?"

I thought it over. "It's been a long time."

"And you want to stop me now?"

"It doesn't feel right."

"It's a stack of dead stuff. Like Wes said it's meat and bones."

He was right. We hardly ever had fun. Removing a head from a pile of body parts to scare Gordy sounded gross and wrong, but it also sounded fun. "Okay, but when we're done, we put the head back."

Tyrone clapped his hands together and smiled. "I can't wait to see his face."

Chapter Four

We decided to spend a few nights in the fire tower. We were cold and tired, and we needed a lot of time to recharge. Finding Lou was a priority, but we weren't going find her if we died from exhaustion.

Gordy had told me a couple of times about the comic book he had read with Lou in it. He was sure it was her. He couldn't say why he hadn't thought of it before, but something just jogged his memory. She was headed to Buffalo. He couldn't remember how or why, but if she made it she died.

"I didn't really read it," he said. "I just remember the way she died. It was totally awesome... I mean it was when I thought it was just a comic book."

"Okay," I said. "How?"

"How what?"

"How did she die, idiot?"

"These things just ripped her apart, man. It was sick. Blood and guts everywhere. It was insanely cool... I mean it was when I thought it was just a comic book."

"What things?" I asked.

He shrugged. "I don't know. They were just these things. Invisible almost. I just remember how they made me feel."

"How?"

He hesitated. "It's weird, but I kind of felt sorry for them. It was almost like they thought they were doing Lou a favor, like she had been begging them to tear her into pieces for a long time, and they just finally broke down and did it because they thought it was cruel not to. Does that make sense?"

"No," I said. "You sure Dr. Bashir wasn't behind her death?"

"He was there... I guess... I mean I didn't really read it. The pictures were pretty awesome. I just kind of looked at those."

I asked him about it every night hoping he'd remember something new, but he hadn't come up with anything new in a week or so. The last thing he remembered was that one of the invisible creatures cried like a baby.

"Creepy, dude. Really creepy," he said.

Chapter Five

Tyrone sneaked the head up to the fire tower in his backpack with my help. I actually felt kind of bad helping him prank Gordy in such a hideous, awful way, but Tyrone was so excited about it that I felt like I had to. He hadn't been even mildly amused, much less excited, since I'd rejoined the group. He'd been an adventurous little kid back when this all started. Of course, that was back when he had Valerie. Without her, he was a sour, scary guy. I really wanted adventurous Tyrone back even if it was at the expense of my best friend Gordy.

I'd be lying if said I wasn't a little excited myself to see Gordy freak out when he found the head. I was mad at myself for feeling that way. I got the idea that since I was the leader I shouldn't be doing kid-stuff, but Gordy was going to flip his lid. How could I not want to be in on that? I only hoped he didn't pee in the sleeping bag. I did not want to have to try to track down another sporting goods store or Walmart or whatever to find another one. The sleeping bags were a pretty rare item in a dead, freezing world.

I distracted Gordy by luring him and Wes out on the deck of the fire tower and getting them to review some maps we had picked up at a ranger's station a few weeks back.

Wes unfolded the map and placed his finger on a spot. "Can't say for sure, but I figure we're here."

I peered over my shoulder to see if Tyrone was ready for us to come back in.

"Where's here?" Gordy asked.

"New Jersey."

Gordy stretched his neck and scanned the wilderness. "New Jersey? But this is like woods and stuff."

"So?" Wes said examining the map.

"I thought New Jersey was a city with buildings and streets and traffic lights and..."

Wes groaned. "Didn't your parents teach you nothing?"

"You should talk Mr. Grammar... whatever, your grammar sucks."

"Grammar ain't gonna do me a lick of good fighting monsters and trying to get by in this new world of ours. But knowing New Jersey is a state that includes forests and wildlife and not just cities and beaches does come in handy."

"Okay, smart guy," Gordy said. "What does being in New Jersey tell you?"

"Tells me we should cut through the Delaware State Forest and head into Scranton. Load up on more supplies and then see if we can find some mode of transportation besides our feet to take us to Buffalo."

I hadn't been paying much attention to their conversation until that point. I looked at the map. "What if Lou didn't go that way?"

Wes snickered. "I ain't a psychic. I don't know which way Lou went."

"We have to follow Lou's trail," I said. "We have to catch up to her before she gets to Buffalo."

Wes put his hand on my shoulder. "Son, you say we've been on Lou's trail for a while now, but I gotta be honest, I haven't seen a sign of her anywhere. I ain't saying I'm giving up on finding her, but I just think we need to concentrate on traveling smart instead of going off half-cocked."

"We have been following her trail," I said.

"How do you know?"

I hesitated because the truth was I didn't know how I knew. There were no signs of her, but I could feel her. "I know it, Wes. She's been everywhere we've been. I wouldn't be surprised if she's been on this deck looking out at these same trees."

I could tell he thought I had lost my mind, but he didn't say it. Maybe I had. "I'm of the mind we should get to Buffalo as quick as possible to see if we can head her off at the pass. We ain't seen a Délon or Bashir or Greasywhopper or Silencer or what have you in weeks. They ain't this far north. It might be safe enough to where we can set up a perimeter on the south entrance to Buffalo. Catch her before she enters the city."

I turned to see Tyrone standing in the doorway. He was fighting to hide a grin. "Cold enough for you?" he asked.

Wes gave him a quick glance and then returned to the map. "It is that."

Tyrone bit his lip to keep from laughing. After a long pause, he managed to say, "Why don't you come inside? It's getting late anyway."

"Late?" Wes surveyed the dark sky that contained just a hint of purple. "I guess it is kind of late." He attempted to fold the map. "We can get back to this in the morning. I'd like to hole up here tomorrow. Maybe even the next day, too."

"That long?" I asked.

He shrugged. "We are worn down to nubs, Oz. We need to lay low for awhile. Fatten up. If we cut through the forest like I said it's bound to be harder traveling than what we've been doing." He shook his head. "But, I ain't the leader. You are. You gotta make the call."

"Guys," Tyrone said excitedly, "let's get some sleep."

"What's wrong with you?" Gordy said with a laugh. "You turn into some scared little girl that can't sleep by herself."

Tyrone hid a smile. "No."

"You're lucky Lou's not here to hear you call someone a scared little girl," I said walking toward the door.

Gordy said in a panic, "It slipped out. Please don't tell her when we find her."

Wes playfully shoved him forward. "You're about three bricks shy of a full load, boy."

We entered the cabin where Tyrone had laid out all the sleeping bags. Gordy's was in the middle. The bulge at the end of his sleeping bag was hidden by his backpack. All the sleeping bags had backpacks at the end of them so it wouldn't look suspicious.

Tyrone quickly climbed into his sleeping bag without moving the pack. "Keeps my feet warmer," he said as he wiggled into a comfortable position.

"I can't sleep with a pack on my feet," Gordy said as he leaned over to move it.

Tyrone stopped him. "Wait!"

We were all a little startled by his panicked tone of voice.

"I'm telling you it'll keep your feet warm. You'll sleep better."

I smiled. "He's right."

"He is?" Gordy asked.

"At least try it," Tyrone said.

I quickly got into my sleeping bag and made a big show about how warm my feet were.

Gordy and Wes shared a look before they followed and climbed into their sleeping bags.

Tyrone and I watched Gordy as he slid into position. We could barely hide our excitement. It was a mean, horrible trick, but it was about to pay off.

Gordy froze. "What…"

Tyrone snickered.

"There's something in my sleeping bag…"

Tyrone slapped the floor a few times.

"What did you put in my bag, Tyrone…" Gordy screamed so loud I thought the fire tower would crumble. He scrambled out of the bag.

Tyrone and I were howling with laughter. I thought I was going to puke I was laughing so hard.

Wes sat up with a start. "What in tarnation is going on?"

"Something bit me!" Gordy said.

I heard him say it, but it didn't register right away. Tyrone was too far gone to hear anything.

"Bit you?" Wes said standing. He looked at Tyrone and me. "What did you two do?"

"I'm bleeding," Gordy said.

I stopped laughing when I saw his foot. He was bleeding.

"Nothing bit you," Tyrone said in between fits of laughter. "You're not bleeding."

"He is bleeding," I said standing.

Tyrone looked at him. "Holy crap!"

We all observed the sleeping bag. The lump was moving, inching its way toward the opening.

"You boys want to tell me what's going on?"

"How is it moving?" Tyrone asked. "It's just a head."

"What's just a head?" Gordy asked.

"I put the head in your sleeping bag. It was just a joke."

"What head?"

"From the forest. The one that was in that pile of body parts."

"What?" Wes asked.

"It was a joke," Tyrone said. "It's just a head."

"Nothing is 'just' around here, son. You oughta know that by now."

We all watched as the lump in the sleeping back continued to move.

"It bit me!" Gordy shouted. "You put a head in my sleeping bag, and it bit me. So help me, if I turn into anything I'm coming after you first, Tyrone! You can count on that!"

"Relax," I said, "you're not going to turn into anything." I hurried to my pack and retrieved a knife. Wes and Tyrone did the same.

"No sense in waiting for it to come out," Wes said. He moved to the foot of the sleeping bag and picked it up. "You boys ready?"

We all nodded except for Gordy. He moved to the other side of the room.

Wes lifted the end of the sleeping bag as high as he could and the head rolled out onto the floor. We all approached with our knives ready.

The head came to a stop on its left ear. Its mouth was opening and closing.

"Good crap in a hat," Wes said.

It shifted its eyes to Wes when it heard his voice. We all jumped back.

"That thing's alive," Gordy said.

"Well," Wes said, "it ain't quite dead. Let's put it that way."

It stuck its tongue out and tried to touch the floor with it.

"It's licking the floor! Make it stop!" Gordy said.

Tyrone bent down to examine it closer. The head shifted its eyes to him. "It's not licking the floor. It's trying to roll on its face."

Wes and I bent in closer.

"What in tarnation for?"

"Check it out," Tyrone said sounding excited once again. "It moves like a snail. When it's on its face, it uses its tongue to move across the floor."

"Oh my God," Gordy said. "I'm going to turn into a snail head!"

"Hush up," Wes said sharply. "You ain't turning into a snail head."

"How do you know that's what it's trying to do?" I asked Tyrone.

"Because," he said with a smile that sent chills down my spine. "That's what I'd do if I was a head."

The head tilted side to side and rolled on its face. Just as Tyrone had said, it used its tongue to crawl along the floor like a snail.

"What were you boys thinking bringing that thing up here?" Wes asked.

"It was a joke," I said.

"A joke? That's a person's head. You don't joke around with a thing like that. Forget that it's alive and scooting across the floor on its own. It's a person that was just like us at one point. It had friends and family and whatnot. That's just plain disrespectful."

Tyrone snickered.

"Son," Wes said stepping towards him, "you need a good whooping is what you need. Carrying on like a lunatic. You're getting more and more off-tilt every day."

Tyrone stood. "Relax, fat…"

I stood and yelled, "Hey!" Stepping in between them I said, "Wes is right. It was stupid…"

"And disrespectful," Wes said staring holes in Tyrone.

"And disrespectful," I said. "This is on me. It's my mistake. I let it happen."

Tyrone shifted his gaze from Wes to me. "You let it happen?"

"I'm the leader. I should have known better. I should have stopped you."

"Stop me? I ain't your puppet. You don't tell me what to do."

Something came over me. I grabbed him by his collar and slammed him against the wall. "I am your leader. That's how it works. You don't like, it you know where the door is."

He worked himself free and tried to kill me with a look of pure hatred.

"Guys," Gordy said.

We all turned to him.

"There's still a head crawling on its tongue across the floor."

I stepped away from Tyrone and watched the head inch its way to the door.

"Any idea what we should do with it?" Wes asked.

"Kill it," Tyrone said.

"Kill it?" Gordy said. "It's already dead, ain't it? Please tell me it's already dead."

"Dead or undead," I said. "You know how things work around here."

"How do you kill something that's already dead? Or undead?" Gordy asked.

"Smash it like a pumpkin," Tyrone said.

"Hold on," Wes said. "We ain't gonna smash it. It just compounds the disrespect, and it's messy as hell."

"We could burn it," I said.

"Burn it?" Wes asked, mulling over the idea. "That ain't no different than cremating a body, I guess."

"We can't burn it," Tyrone said.

"And why not?" Wes asked

"Because I visited a crematorium once when I was little. With my Grandfather. The guy that worked there said the fire has to be like 1800 degrees or something. That's a lot hotter than we can build a fire."

"Dude," Gordy said, "you're grandfather took you to a crematorium?"

Tyrone waved him off. "Long story."

"Okay, so we can't burn it, and we can't smash it. What do we do with it?" Wes asked.

Ariabod and Ajax had been signing to each other the whole time we were talking. They'd even shared a few grins. Finally, Ariabod knuckle walked over to the head, grabbed it by the hair, and tossed it out the door and over the deck. He shook his head in disgust and walked back to Ajax.

"I suppose we could just toss it outside," Wes said holding back a laugh.

Chapter Six

The first thing I noticed when I woke up the next morning was that Tyrone was gone. The others, gorillas and humans alike, were all still asleep. I stepped out on the deck into a light snowfall. Looking past the railing to the ground below, I saw a fresh set of footprints leading into the woods.

I bundled up as quickly and as quietly as I could, hurried down the steps and followed the prints. I wasn't all that surprised to see Tyrone staring into the dome-shaped shelter of sticks.

"You put it back?" I asked when I spotted the head back in the pile with the other body parts.

Without turning, he said, "Found it this way."

"Wait? It crawled up there itself?"

He shrugged. "I don't know. I doubt it, but I can't say for sure one way or the other. "

I stood next to him. "If it didn't crawl there itself, that means there's someone else around here."

"Or something else," he said.

I nodded.

We both stared at the pile of mismatched parts without saying a word. The snow floated over the tops of the trees and covered the bare limbs.

Finally, Tyrone said, "If you laid these parts out on the ground, you could piece together a person."

"A person?" I pointed to the rib cage that was partially covered in fur. "That's some kind of animal."

He agreed. "I'm not saying it would look like a regular person. I'm saying there's parts in there for two legs with two feet, two arms with hands, a chest, a head. All the parts you need to build a human-like creature of some kind."

I scanned the pile. He was right. It would make an ugly, deformed human-like creature, but it would make one. Peering through the cracks I could even see internal organs: a heart, guts, detached muscles. It was just a pile of yuck.

"Still doesn't explain how the head got back up there," I said.

"Wasn't trying to explain anything. Just telling you what I see." He looked the way we came. "If someone or something put it back on the pile, the snow must have covered up their tracks."

I examined the path. "We need to be on our toes until we leave," I said. "We'll post lookouts from here on out."

He nodded.

I cleared my throat not really wanting to bring up what had happened the night before, but I had to. "We need to talk about last night."

"What about it?" he asked still fixated on the pile.

"We were wrong."

He didn't saying anything.

"And you were out of line."

He still didn't say anything. He just stared at the stupid pile.

I searched the ground and found eight sticks that were roughly the same size. I moved around in front of him and handed him one of the sticks. "Break this," I said.

He looked at me intently before taking the stick. With little effort, he snapped it in half.

I handed him the remaining sticks. "Now break these all at once."

He held the bundle of sticks and tried with all his strength to break them, but he couldn't do it. After a few seconds of struggling, he handed them back to me and said, "Can't."

I held up the sticks. "This is us, Tyrone. We're these seven sticks. Together we can't be broken." I removed one stick from the group and broke it. "Alone we're dead. We need to be on the same page. This whole leader thing annoys the crap out of me. I didn't ask for it, but that's what it's come down to. You're the strongest one in our group. You can out-muscle me, out-quick Wes, out-anything Gordy, and out-think the apes. This doesn't work without you. Understand?"

He shrugged. "I just don't like being told what to do."

I nodded. "I get that. Neither do I, but you're looking at it all wrong. We're not six separate people... well, five people and two apes." I turned to the pile. "We're one group... one person. We have to work together to survive."

"Five people? There're only four…"

"You're forgetting Lou."

He nodded. "So, if we're all body parts for the same body, that makes you the head with the brain, right?"

I considered his question. "More or less."

He cocked an eyebrow. “What’s that make me?”

I grabbed one of his hands and folded his fingers into a tight little ball. “You’re the fists.”

A smile slowly formed on his face. “I’m the fists.” He opened and closed both hands, and his smile got bigger. “I am the fists.”

Chapter Seven

"We need to do a little scouting," Wes said munching on a small bag of peanut M&Ms. "Maybe go off in twos. Since we come up from the South, we can head out North, East, and West."

"What for?" Gordy asked massaging his injured foot.

Wes wadded up the empty M&Ms wrapper and tossed it aside. "We're running low on everything. We ain't got but three knives and one crossbow between us. How many arrows we got, Tyrone?"

Tyrone held up two fingers.

"That ain't gonna cut it."

"How far out do you want to scout?" I asked.

Wes titled his head from right to left as he thought about the question. "With this weather, I'd say no more than a mile, maybe a mile and a half."

I nodded. "You take Ajax and head east. Gordy's with me. We'll head north, and Tyrone's got Ariabod."

"Let me guess," Tyrone said. "You want us to go west."

"You're psychic," I said gathering together supplies for the hike.

Gordy pointed to his foot. "Hello, injured, remember?"

"Put your boots on," Wes said standing. "That snail head barely broke the skin, you big baby."

"It still made me bleed," Gordy said sounding disappointed that he wasn't getting any sympathy.

"You've been bit before," Wes said. "And a whole lot worse."

Gordy threw up his hands. "I know! I'm always the one getting bit! What's up with that?" He made a big show of demonstrating how much it hurt putting on his boot.

Wes whistled to Ajax. "Let's go, go-rilla."

Ajax grunted and followed Wes out the door.

Tyrone tossed me the crossbow. "Take it. I got my fists," he said with a grin. He and Ariabod exited the fire tower.

Ten minutes passed before Gordy was ready to go. He whined the whole time. I gave serious consideration to tossing him over the deck once we got outside.

"You never did apologize," Gordy said as we took our first step into the forest.

"About what?"

"About what?" he said sounding disgusted. "The head. In my sleeping bag. Remember?"

"Oh," I said. "That. I guess I should apologize."

"No kidding. You almost killed me. Me... your best friend."

"You're right. I'm sorry. It was stupid."

"And mean."

"And mean," I said. "But, since it appears you're going to live, I have to admit it was kind of funny."

"Appears I'm going to live? Are you saying there's still a chance I won't?"

I laughed. "Man, Gordy you need to get a grip…" I stopped suddenly. Ahead of us, through some thick brush, there was another shelter made of sticks.

Gordy saw what I was staring at and asked, "Did we go the wrong way?" He looked over his shoulder.

"No," I said.

"But how did that thing get over here?"

"It didn't."

His eyes opened wide. "It's another one?"

I nodded and moved towards the domed shaped shelter. We were nearly on top of it when we saw the pile of body parts. It was stacked as neat at the other one, but the parts came from a different jumble of animals and people.

"Deer head," Gordy said pointing.

"Baby hands," I said.

"Baby hands?" Gordy asked, trying to see through the decaying flesh and broken bones. "Oh man. Those are baby hands. Like from a real baby."

We moved in closer to get a better look.

"Let's go back," Gordy said.

"We haven't even gone 100 yards."

"No, I mean back south. Let's get away from these things. Let's just keep walking until we're back in Tullahoma."

"Can't. Not without Lou."

"I don't know why you're so worried about Lou," he said. "She's the bad-assiest one of us all. She can take care of herself. We're the ones that need her. She doesn't need us."

"First, bad-assiest isn't a word and, second, if we go back south there are tons of Destroyers waiting for us."

"I don't care. I'd rather deal with them than these ugly piles of legs and heads and... just downright disgusting crap."

"They don't do anything. They don't even move."

Gordy held out his foot. "Hello, one of them bit me."

"Yes, but it wouldn't have... that was our fault... you know…" I didn't really know how to answer him. He was right. It did move, but I still didn't think it was a threat. What can a pile of body parts do? I just didn't know how to explain it to Gordy. "Let's finish looking around, or do you want to be caught out in the woods at night with this thing?"

He grimaced and stomped ahead of me.

I gave the pile one last glance and moved on. There wasn't much of a path for us to follow. The snow wasn't as deep as it was outside the forest, but the lack of light made it icier. The only way to travel without falling every other step was to grab hold of trees and pull ourselves forward. Thirty or so minutes passed, and we could still see the domed shelter.

"This is crazy," Gordy said. "We're not going to find anything out here."

I had an idea he was right, but that didn't change what had to be done. "Maybe, but there's only one way to know for sure."

"I thought we were supposed to be resting. This isn't resting." He put his hands on his knees and bent over to catch his breath.

"You complain more than…" I stopped when I saw smoke streaming over the tree tops.

"More than what?" Gordy asked. He saw me with my chin pointing up as I tried to determine where the smoke was coming from. "Whoa."

The wind was blowing the smoke towards us. "Let's go," I said carefully moving ahead of Gordy.

"Go? Towards the smoke?"

"We came out here to see if anything was out here, didn't we?" I pointed to the smoke. "Something's out here."

Gordy became panic-stricken. "Okay, so something's out here. Now we know. Let's go back and tell the others."

"Gordy, you either come with me, or I will knock you out and drag you with me."

He growled. "You're so damn bossy!" He reluctantly followed.

It wasn't long before we could smell the smoke. It wasn't just wood that was burning. There was the distinct odor of meat cooking over an open fire.

We reached a grouping of three large trees and stopped. Just past a thin line of smaller trees, we saw a lodge. It was made of heavy stones with a wood shingled roof. Smoke puffed out its chimney like a train coming down the tracks.

A man stepped out the door of the little house and awkwardly picked up a small stack of wood.

"Let's go," Gordy said.

I shook my head. "You stay here. I'm going to try to find a window. I want to see inside."

"Why? It's a creepy guy cooking dinner. We don't need to see anymore."

"What makes you think he's creepy?"

"Dude," he worked hard not to yell out in frustration. "Everyone is creepy in this place."

I motioned for him to stay put, and loaded the crossbow. Slowly I moved around the woods until I could approach the lodge from the back. I stooped down next to a large tree and watched for any signs of life before I decided it was safe to approach the small building. Once I reached it, I stepped lightly to the far corner opposite the chimney and spotted a small window.

I pressed myself against the stone wall and inched my way towards it. I took a quick peek inside and backed way quickly. Confidant that no one inside could see me, I leaned to the right and took my first good long peek inside.

It was a single small room. There were a couple of cots near the fireplace. Clothes and trash littered the floor. The man stacked the wood he'd retrieved from the front next to the door. The window was covered with dirt and grime, so it was hard to make out every detail, but there was something off about him. He was moving strangely.

When he took off his coat, it was clear what was wrong with him. He was missing a hand, and a leg, and it appeared like he was using the butt of a rifle as a fake leg. He threw a small log on the fire and then walked to one of the cots. He struggled to bend down and keep his balance. When he stood back up he was holding something black and slimy. He hobbled over to the fire and tossed it in the flames.

I heard a noise behind me and turned quickly. A small boy in an oversized coat and flannel hunting cap stared back at me.

"Hi," I said in a whisper.

He didn't reply.

"Is this your house?"

He stood motionless with a blank expression.

"Is that your dad inside?"

He shook his head.

"What are you doing out here?"

He held out his hand and showed me what he was holding: a human foot that was covered in dried blood with the ankle bone still attached.

I suddenly found it hard to catch a clean breath.

"Walk this way, minnow," I heard a voice say.

The one-legged man stood at the corner of the lodge. He had a knife in his hand and his eyes on me.

"My name's Oz," I said nervously.

"I don't care," the man said. "Minnow, over here now!"

"I'm not here for trouble," I said.

"You're here. That's trouble enough."

"I'm just passing through with my friends…"

"Friends?" He took a clumsy step forward. "Minnow! Get over here now!"

The kid ran to the one-legged man.

"Get out of here," the man said to me. "You and your friends. Get as far from this place as you can."

"We are. We're just resting for a few days…"

"Resting? You picked a bad place to do that. Get! Head south! Get out of the cold."

"South? We're going north to Buffalo."

Minnow hid himself behind the man who was laughing like a lunatic. "North? They're migrating north, jackass. You need to go south."

I kept my eyes on the boy. "We just came from the south. It's not safe."

He pushed the boy further behind him.

"What's migrating north?" I asked.

The one-legged man shifted towards the house but lost his footing. He stumbled to the ground losing his grip on his knife in the process. As I approached to help, I realized I didn't exactly win his trust by holding a loaded crossbow.

The man scrambled for the knife.

"I'm not going to hurt you." Stopping I said, "Look," as I carefully placed the crossbow on the ground.

He reached the knife and rolled over on his back gripping it tightly. "Get out of here!"

"Are you okay?"

He laughed again. "No, I'm not okay. Do I look okay? I got one leg and one hand off."

"Let me help you," I said skulking towards him.

"Why?"

"Because you need some help."

"No, I mean why do you want to help me? What's in it for you? We don't have food to share. You can't sleep in the cabin. And I'm not interested in making any new friends. A new friend is how I got this way."

"We don't have to be friends," I said. "I'm happy to walk away, but you're in a pretty tough spot, and you're not doing the boy much good at the moment."

"I can manage. I fall all the time. Don't you worry about Minnow."

We heard twigs snap and watched Gordy step out of the tree line. "Oz?"

The man shifted on his back to get a better view of the new stranger walking out of the woods. "I see how it is. There are two of you now. You here to rob us? You gonna take food and supplies from a crippled man and a small boy?"

I shook my head. "Wow, you have some serious trust issues, mister. That's my friend Gordy. He's harmless if you want to know the truth. Annoying but harmless."

"Hey," Gordy said. "I'm not that annoying."

Ignoring him I said, "There are four more in our group."

"But two of them are gorillas," Gordy added. "The monkey kind not the war kind."

The man sat up and eased his grip on the knife. "You're traveling with gorillas?"

I watched as Gordy approached with a confused expression on his face. "Doesn't everybody?"

The tension eased from the man's face. "Why didn't you say so?" He gave the knife to Minnow and then reached his hand out towards me. "What're you waiting for? Help me up."

Gordy and I helped him to his foot and rifle butt. Minnow held onto the knife by the blade, pinching it between his thumb and finger while still holding onto the mangled foot with his other hand. As soon as the man was standing, he took the knife from the boy, and we all went into the cabin. Minnow tossed the foot into the fireplace and wiped the blood on his pants.

"Name's, Vance," the man said. "Michael Vance if you want the full name. Can't imagine that sort of thing matters these days, full names and such."

"I'm…" I started, but he interrupted.

"Oz and he's Gordy the annoying. You told me."

"It's just you and Minnow?" I asked.

"It is now," he said. "We had a gorilla, too. Ron."

"Ron?" Gordy said with a smile. "Your gorilla's name was Ron."

Vance didn't see the humor in the name. "What's wrong with Ron? Ron's a good name."

"But for a gorilla?"

"What're your gorillas' names?'

"Ajax and Ariabod."

Vance's eyes opened wide, and it took him a few minutes to compose himself. "Ajax?"

Gordy and I shared a look.

"The Ajax?" Vance asked as he approached.

Confused I answered, "I guess."

He got Minnow's attention and said loudly, "They know Ajax." He repeated 'Ajax' several times, each time using exaggerated mouth movements. Turning back to us, "You're really with Ajax?"

Gordy rolled his eyes. "What's the big deal about Ajax?"

"What's the big deal?" Vance asked. He laughed and slapped his remaining leg. Turning to Minnow he said, "They don't know who Ajax is. Can you believe it? They're with Ajax, and they don't even know who he is…" He waved the boy off. "Ah, you can't hear a word I'm saying."

He hobbled over to a backpack and pulled out four full-sized Hershey's chocolate bars. After tossing one to the boy, he held out two for us to take.

Gordy reached for it, but I stopped him.

"We're not here to take your supplies. We've got plenty."

Vance insisted. "This is a celebration! Besides I know where to get tons more."

I hesitated and then nodded to Gordy. He snatched the two chocolate bars from Vance and immediately ripped one open.

"Holy crap," he said chewing with a chocolate caked smile. "This so beats those granola thingies."

"Maybe you should tell us what you know about Ajax," I said to Vance.

He munched on his Hershey's bar. "Your Ajax is just about the most important person left on this planet... Well, I guess he's not the most important person because he's not a person. He's the most important…"

Gordy bit into his chocolate bar again. "Monkey?"

"He's not a monkey," I said. "He's an ape."

"Same thing, dude."

"Whatever he is, he's important," Vance said. "And there's nobody or nothing more important. I thought he was a myth if you want to know the truth. Met a girl a few weeks ago who claimed to know him. Said he was real. But I didn't believe her. She was a little nutty. But, now that you say you're with him.... wait a minute, you're not wackos, too, are you?"

"What girl," I said excitedly. "What was her name? What did she look like?"

He bit into his chocolate bar. "Some girl."

I slapped the candy out of his hand. "What girl?"

He stepped back on his fake leg.

"Whoa, whoa, whoa," Gordy said pulling me back. "The guy knows where to get chocolate. Let's not piss him off. Listen... Mark…"

"Michael, but nobody calls me that. They call me Vance."

"Okay, Vance, you'll have to excuse my friend Oz. You see, we've been searching for a girl. She used to be a part of our group, but we got separated."

"Is she crazy?"

Gordy shook his head. "She's more of a bad-ass warrior type."

"Her name's Lou," I said. "Or she may be going by Emily Bristol."

Minnow picked up Vance's candy bar and handed it back to him. "Can't help you out on a name. She said she didn't have one. I told you she was wacko."

"What did she look like?" Oz asked.

Vance shrugged. "Can't say for sure."

I groaned. "What do you mean you can't say? Are you blind?"

He smiled, revealing chocolate-covered teeth. "I am as close to it as you can get without being blind. Used to wear contacts that corrected my vision enough to get by, but I ran out, and my glasses broke about a month before I met up with your crazy girl and her crazy friend. Shapes are the best I can do. I couldn't even tell you the color of her hair."

"So," Gordy said, "you've got one hand, one leg, and you can't see. How are you still alive?"

Vance winked. "Just lucky I guess."

"What did this girl say?" I asked.

"Not a whole lot that's worth repeating. She bleated on about some boy she was in love with. Talked about missing her friends. Said something about comic books and Storytellers and blah, blah, blah. Crazy talk."

I smiled at Gordy. "That's Lou. It has to be."

"Sounds like her."

"When was the last time you saw her?"

Vance thought about the question. "Let me see. I'd say it's been a week maybe ten days. They bleed together so I can't say for certain.

Minnow stood in front of the fire and stared at the flames.

"The boy misses her. I can tell you that. She looked after him. Saved his life. Saved mine. Crazy or not, she was a good gal."

I nodded. "Yes, she is."

"That man she's with. He's trouble. He'll get her killed if she ain't dead already."

"What man?"

Vance limped to the cot and sat down. "What was his name?" He closed his eyes tightly. "My memory's a little sketchy sometimes."

"Geez," Gordy said, "you've got a lot of problems."

I elbowed Gordy in the ribs, and he nearly spit out his last bite of chocolate.

"That I do, young fella. That I do... you are young, aren't you? You sound young, but you could be older than me for all I know."

"I ain't as old as you," Gordy said. "We got a guy in our group who might be your age. He's fat."

Vance giggled. "Now there's something I thought I'd never come across again, a fat person. Not with the way things are. Everything being scarce and all."

I tried not to show my frustration, but I was getting impatient. "The man that was with Lou; do you remember his name?"

"No…" he snapped his fingers. "Frank was his name." He snarled. "I hate that guy like I've never hated anyone in my life. Frank. Frank. Frank…" He furrowed his brow. "Wait, was that his name?"

Minnow stoked the fire with a long thick stick. The foot was nearly engulfed by the flames.

"So, what's with the kid burning a foot?"

Vance inspected the fire with squinted eyes. "You got a foot, Minnow?"

The boy didn't respond.

"You can't hear me," Vance said waving him off. "What do you expect us to do with all these body parts?"

Gordy said, "How about nothing?"

"You do nothing, and there will be trouble," Vance said. "Big, gigantic loads of trouble." He removed the rifle butt and scratched the end of his stub. "Then again, burning them causes some trouble, too. They come looking for them, but they're easier to handle if you take the human parts. They're all thumbs without their human parts." He cracked up when he realized what he had said. "All thumbs! I made a joke without trying!"

"That was your idea of a joke?" Gordy asked.

I sat down next to Vance on the cot. "Are you saying the piles of body parts come to life?"

He shook his head. "They don't come to life. They are alive."

"How is that possible?" I asked. "They don't even go together. It's just a hodgepodge of different... things. They're all just stacked there in a pile."

Vance giggled. "That's their trick. That's the way they get you to think you're safe. They're just useless piles of dead limbs and heads and hearts and brains. But they are alive, and they can move. Trust me. They can move like you wouldn't believe."

"We've seen it," Gordy said. His attention was on the fire and watching the foot burn.

"We have?" I asked.

He lifted up his foot. "Remember the head you put in my sleeping bag? The one that bit me? Jerk."

Vance's face went from a smile to a frown and he scrambled to get his leg back on. "You got bit?"

Gordy stepped back with a worried expression on his face. "Yeah. Why? Is that bad?"

"What do you think? You got bit by an undead head, an undead head that belongs to the Gore!"

"The Gore? You see?" Gordy shouted. "I knew getting bit was bad! I'm going to turn into something, aren't I? I'm going to be an undead... thing. Oh my God, my body's going to fall apart. I'm going to be stuck in one of the piles... a bunch of those piles. I'll be scattered all over the place…"

Vance doubled over, snorting and guffawing like nobody's business. When he could catch his breath, he said, "I'm just messing with you, kid."

Gordy appeared as if he'd been punched in the stomach. "You are? Really?"

"Of course! I do that! Ask Minnow, he'll tell you... on second thought don't ask him. He can't hear a thing."

"Oh my God," Gordy said holding his hand over his heart. "Oh my God. I'm not going to die or un-die or whatever you call it."

"Oh, they may still get you, but you won't turn into anything until they kill you first."

The horrified look returned to Gordy's face.

"They'll most likely kill the whole lot of you. You desecrated it. Taking the head is frowned upon in their culture. Not as bad as taking the hands, but the head riles them up."

"I didn't take the head," Gordy said. "Butt-brain sitting next to you did."

"It's true," I said with a nod.

"Well it was a foolish thing to do," Vance said. "Foolish, foolish, foolish... Floyd was that guy's name, not Frank!" He said excitedly shifting gears.

"Floyd?" I asked. "The cook?"

Vance appeared surprised. "You know him?"

"Yes," I said. "We do."

Vance reattached his fake leg. "Well, he is not to be trusted. I will tell you that. That girl of yours has hitched her wagon to a mess of double trouble. He has got her deep into something nobody should be a part of." He stood. "Now, if you'll excuse me, I've got to get ready for are little party."

"Party?" I asked.

"You say the boy brought back a foot?"

"Yes."

"The owner of that foot will be coming around shortly to get it back. I've got to be ready by the time it gets here."

I stood. "We'll help you."

"We will?" Gordy asked. "Listen, I'm all for meeting new people and making new friends, but I don't see why we need to stick around to fight some freaky body part monster because the kid screwed up and stole his foot."

"He didn't screw up," Vance said. "That's what he was supposed to do."

"You send him out in the woods to steal body parts from the piles?" I asked.

"I don't so much as send him as he goes on his own without asking. He's pretty damn good at it."

"Wait, you want these…" Gordy stopped because he couldn't remember what Vance had called them earlier.

"They're called the Gore. That's what Floyd named them."

"So you want the Gore to come here."

"Not all of them. I just want the one that's missing a foot. The boy and I can handle that one, especially since he'll be approaching with a considerable limp."

Gordy snickered.

"What's so funny?" Vance asked.

"Don't you have a considerable limp?"

Vance was insulted. "Don't you worry about me. I can take care of myself."

"No offense," I said. "But, Gordy's got a point. You didn't do too well with us out there."

"I'm not dead, am I?" He walked over to the corner next to the fire place and retrieved a pitchfork. "Besides I got Minnow."

Gordy and I both looked at the kid and then at each other before snickering.

"You go ahead and laugh," Vance said walking over to the boy and tapped him on the shoulder. Then, he hit the floor twice with the handle of the pitchfork.

Minnow ran to a backpack and retrieved a ten-inch hunting knife. It appeared ridiculously big in his small hand.

"You should really let us help," I said following them to the door.

"Tell you what. You can watch if you shut up," Vance said.

I threw my hands up in the air. "Whatever you say."

Gordy and I followed them to the edge of the small lodge. I gripped the crossbow tightly. A long, low groan came out of the woods at the other side of the clearing. Vance and Minnow walked another fifty feet.

Quickly, the boy bent down and cleared away some snow and then lay down in the area where he had been digging. Vance adjusted the hood of Minnow's coat so it covered nearly his whole face. When he had it just right, he covered the rest of Minnow in snow.

"What're they doing?" Gordy asked.

"I have no idea," I said stepping forward to get a better view. You wouldn't know there was a boy buried in the snow unless you were right on top of him.

Something stepped out of the woods on the other side of the clearing. It stood on two legs made of parts from various animals. Its human hands hung past its knees. Its arms were bulky collections of more animal parts. Its broad body was patched together with parts from animals and humans. Its head belonged to a nine point buck.

"Holy crap," Gordy said grabbing my arm and pulling me back.

Vance stomped through the snow a few feet in front of the hidden Minnow. He raised his pitchfork and yelled, "I burned your foot you ugly piss-turd!"

The creature lifted its buck head and let out a screech that echoed across the clearing.

"C'mon, you stinking Gore! Come get it!"

The large pieced together monster took a step and screeched again. It rumbled forward with a limp through the deep snow.

"That's it, come and get me!"

The Gore used its hands to help it move faster through the snow. It was moving both frantically and awkwardly because it only had one foot.

I quickly started to get the crossbow ready.

The Gore was closing in fast.

"Almost here, Minnow!" Vance shouted.

I moved forward.

"What are you doing?" Gordy asked.

"I can't just stand here and do nothing."

"Yes, you can," Gordy said. "I'm doing it. It's easy."

The Gore was just a few feet away from Vance when he thrust the pitchfork into its pink pig belly. The creature bellowed and snorted. Vance leaned into the pitchfork and roared.

I fired the crossbow and hit the Gore just above its right eye. It shook its head violently. Vance lost his grip on the pitchfork and stumbled to the left until he completely lost his footing and fell on his side.

"I told you to just watch!" Vance said struggling to stand.

The Gore spun toward him.

"Get him over the boy!" Vance said in a panic.

"What?"

"Do it!"

I hesitated and then whistled to get the Gore's attention. "Over here! Deer head, over here!"

The Gore whirled around clumsily.

I hurried to stand in front of Minnow. "This way!"

The Gore growled and changed his direction to head towards me. It stomped and dragged its footless leg. It repeated the clumsy walk until it straddled Minnow.

"What now?" I asked Vance.

"Give it a second," Vance said.

"Give what a second…"

Like a bullet leaving the barrel of a gun, Minnow leapt out of the snow, climbed up the Gore and stuck the huge knife where the buck head attached to the rest of the body, and he sliced it free. He fell to the ground holding onto the antlers, dropped the head and removed the right hand of the Gore in a flash. I had never seen anyone move so fast.

The headless Gore wobbled in a circle waving its handless arm in the air.

"Told you," Vance said standing. "I got Minnow."

The boy continued to cut the Gore into pieces.

Chapter Eight

After Minnow had completely disassembled the Gore, we all carried the pieces into the lodge and burned the creature piece by piece.

Vance held up one of the hands. "All of them have these."

"Hands?" Gordy asked.

"Not just hands, human hands. No ape hands or bear paws or cow hooves. They all have human hands." He tossed it into the fire. He then held up the stub where his hand used to be. "One of them got mine."

"Your leg, too?" I asked.

"Yep. More or less."

"More or less?" Gordy asked.

"They got it, but they didn't take it." He stretched his back and moved to the cot. "That Floyd is the one that took my leg. I hate that guy." He sat down.

Gordy looked at him wide-eyed. "Good thing Wes sent him on his way."

I nodded.

"Who's Wes?"

"The fat guy we told you about," Gordy said.

"Oh," Vance said lying back on the cot. "Well, he may be fat, but if he chased Floyd off, he's smart." He closed his eyes.

I hesitated and said, "You should come with us. You and Minnow, I mean."

Vance opened one eye. "Nope."

"But it's not safe. You're surrounded by those Gore things."

"That's nothing new."

"We're up in the fire tower. Off the ground. It's safer."

He snickered. "Safer? If you call being trapped safer, I guess you're right."

I sighed. "We're with Ajax."

He opened both eyes and lifted his head. "I didn't consider that."

"You never did tell us why Ajax is so important," Gordy said.

Vance sat up. His eyes darted about the room as he considered his next move. "I met a man before this all started... a homeless guy. He used to beg for money outside my office building. I must've passed him every workday for a year. He talked about the end of the world, monsters, the dead, the undead, he talked about it all and every bit of what he said happened. Every bit."

"And he talked about Ajax?" I asked.

Vance paused. "Once." He stood and limped to a backpack. "It was the day I gave him five dollars." He chuckled. "It was the only time I ever gave him a red cent. I passed him a thousand times or more and all I ever gave him was five lousy dollars. Can you believe that?"

Neither Gordy nor I responded.

"Anyway, I handed him the five, and he almost cried. He grabbed hold of my hand and pulled me in. Scared the crap out of me at the time. He was desperate for me to hear what he had to say." Vance started digging through his backpack.

"What did he say?" I asked, losing patience.

"I wrote it down," Vance said. "I'm not sure why. I just felt like the wording was important." He let out an "Ah-ha!" when he found a piece a paper. He frantically unfolded it. He peered at the paper and then growled. "Damn it! I can't read a word with these crap eyes of mine." He handed it to me. "Read it."

I took the paper and began to read.

"Out loud!" Vance said. "It's been a while since I heard it myself."

I complied. "The end is almost here. All that is left to feel is fear. The end is almost come. Take the word of this old bum. The end is where you will find your way. It will not bring your final day. The end is where you'll lose to an axe. It is where you find Ajax. He is the siliverbacked king of the simians. He is the path to new beginnings."

Gordy groaned. "Worst poem ever."

Vance took the paper from me. "Maybe, but the guy was dead on. The world ended. I found my calling killing Gore. And I lost my hand to an axe."

"Well, I know Ajax. He's nice for a gorilla, but he ain't no king," Gordy said.

Vance frowned and then waved Gordy off. "You wouldn't know a king if he knighted you."

"So come with us to the fire tower," I said. "You can meet Ajax."

He nodded. "We'll go, but not through the woods."

"What are you going to do, fly?" Gordy asked.

Vance bent down and pulled back a trap door. "Kind of the opposite of that actually."

Gordy and I both inched our way to the opening and peered down. The looks on our faces must have indicated our feelings because Vance asked us if we were scared.

"We just haven't had the best of luck with caves," I said.

"It's not a cave," Vance said. "It's a tunnel."

"Same difference," Gordy said.

"Well, you can go through the woods if you want, but I'm taking the tunnel. The Gore start stirring at dusk and it's coming up quick. If we don't make it out of the woods by nightfall, you can kiss your pretty little hands goodbye."

Vance loaded up Minnow with as many supplies as he could handle. The kid was weighted down with a backpack that was nearly as big as him, a small axe, and a canteen. I tried to take some of the stuff from him, but he scooted down the ladder of the tunnel before I could ask twice.

Once Vance put on his backpack and grabbed his pitchfork, Gordy and I followed him down the ladder. The tunnel wasn't homemade. It was made of concrete and steel.

"Forestry service must have built it," Vance said handing us glow sticks. "Bend and shake. They'll stay lit for thirty minutes or so."

We moved through the tunnel at a slow pace with Minnow leading the way until we reached a section that opened up into a little room. Vance pulled the kid back and stepped in front of him. "They stay out of the tunnels most of the time," he said. "It's always dark down here. That can't sleep in the dark, and they need their sleep or they'll fall apart. Literally fall apart."

"Most of the time?" Gordy asked in a whisper.

"The dumber ones don't always make the best decisions," Vance said slowly moving his glow stick around the small room to light it up.

"How is it a guy who can really only make out shapes can make it through these tunnels?" I asked.

"Wasn't easy at first. Took me a while to get a feel for the drafts and smells down here. They will tell you where you are most the time. I can scoot through this place as fast as my peg leg lets me now. It's easier for me to navigate my way around down here than it is up top."

We heard a whimpering come from a corner of the room behind a rack of metal shelves.

"There's a dumb one," Vance said pointing to something on the floor near the rack.

We all approached with our glow sticks held in front of us. Piece by piece, we revealed the scattered body parts of a Gore.

"General rule is the smaller the head, the dumber the Gore," Vance said moving in for a closer look. He reached down and picked something up. "And I'd say this is a pretty small head." He held up a coyote's head. The mouth opened and let out the same whimpering we had heard earlier.

"You mean one of those big things was walking around with that head?" Gordy asked with a snicker.

"They take what they can get. This one must've come down here hunting for a substitute head. Probably smelled us and got confused." He dropped it on the floor and crushed it with the rifle butt. The sound of the skull smashing and brains bursting was sickening.

"How did it get down here?" I asked.

He stretched the glow stick as far as his arm would allow and showed us an adjoining tunnel. "It's a friggin' maze down here. Tunnels basically go in every direction. I've counted a half dozen entrances…" He stopped midsentence when he spotted something in the darkness. Looking at Gordy he said, "Don't move."

Gordy stiffened. "Dude, don't say 'don't move' in a dark tunnel…"

"There's something on your shoulder... I think," he said squinting. "Damn these eyes."

Something clearly moved on Gordy's shoulder.

"I see it, too," I said.

Gordy couldn't contain himself anymore. He twirled around and screamed. "Get it off! Get it off! Get it off!"

Whatever it was fell to the floor, and I stooped down with my glow stick in front of me. A tiny hand quickly crawled towards me. I yelped and backed away.

Minnow stabbed it through with a knife just before it reached my foot. He held it up while it wriggled wildly at the end of the blade.

Vance cackled.

"Why are things always so insane?" Gordy said fighting against the urge to weep.

Vance examined the hand. "Poor thing had little toddler hands. It needed a whole new set of parts." He scanned the floor.

"What are you doing?" I asked, trying but failing to sound calmer than Gordy. "Shouldn't we go?"

"Well, I'd like to find the other one. Don't want it to sneak into one of our bags. That's trouble we don't want."

"There's another one?" Gordy asked.

"Hell, I will admit to being an exception to the rule, but most of the time one hand does come with another."

Gordy scooted back letting out little whimpering sounds. He held his glow stick out searching for the hand in a panic.

Minnow tugged on my pant leg and pointed at Gordy's other shoulder. I almost laughed when I saw what he was pointing at. There, perched like a parrot on a pirate, was the other hand.

When Gordy saw Minnow and me staring at him, he said, "What?"

Vance stopped and stood up straight.

"Don't move," I said approaching him slowly.

Gordy's brow furrowed. "Why do you people keep saying that?" He tensed up.

"I mean it this time, Gordy. Just stand still." I quickly reached out and grabbed the hand. I could feel it moving and fighting against my grip. I found myself hoping that it didn't have a mouth and teeth to bite me.

Vance laughed again. "You must be sweet as syrup, son. That thing sure does like you."

"What do I do with this?" I asked, struggling to keep control of the little hand.

Vance shrugged. "Well, if we were top side, we'd throw it in the fire. I say throw it down and stomp on it."

"You say?" I asked.

"Hell, this ain't an exact science. This is killing things that shouldn't be alive."

I took a deep breath and threw the hand down on the ground as hard as I could. It hit the concrete floor with a thwack and appeared stunned by the force of the blow. Before I could move into crush it beneath my boot,

Minnow jumped on it with both feet. The cracking of the hand's bones echoed through the small chamber.

Vance giggled. "What can I say? The kid loves killing Gore."

We continued down the corridor that led to the fire tower. Vance was moving as fast as he could. His rifle butt leg made a double click, one when it hit the ground and one when he pressed forward to lift it off the ground. I focused on that click-click until we reached another ladder.

"Fire tower," Vance said. "Comes out at the tree line to the west of the tower. "

I reached for the ladder, but Vance stopped me.

"Let the kid go first."

"I'm not going to…"

"He knows the Gore better than anyone on this dead planet. What you saw today is nothing compared to what he's capable of. He's like a little freaky superhero baby or something."

I hesitated but backed away from the ladder. Minnow stepped in front of me biting down on the blade of his knife. He climbed the ladder and opened the trap door just a crack. He silently worked his way through the opening and gently closed the door. Minutes passed.

"What are we supposed to do?" I asked.

"Wait," Vance said eyeballing the door.

"For what?"

"The signal."

"What signal?"

We heard three quick taps followed by a long pause and then a fourth tap.

"That signal," Vance said climbing up the ladder. "Just because he gave us the all clear doesn't mean we can throw a party. Make as little noise as possible and don't open the door all the way. They can sense the smallest change."

Gordy pushed his way in front of me and put his foot on the bottom rung of the ladder. "Let me go first to see if it's safe," he said with a grin.

I grinned back and watched him climb. When he was at the top of the ladder, I waited until he crawled through the tiny opening of the door before I started to climb. Two rungs up, I heard a noise coming down the corridor. I strained to see through the darkness of the tunnel, but it was impossible. I held out my glow stick as far as it would go, but it didn't help. Finally, I tossed the stick down the tunnel as far as I could. It bounced off the wall and rolled along the ground a good distance. A human hand attached to large fur covered arm reached out of the darkness and picked it up. The glow stick illuminated a human face that was more skeleton than anything else. I barked out a short scream and scrambled up the ladder. With no regard for noise, I burst through the trap door and shouted, "Close it! Close it! Close it!" I dove into a snow bank and turned on my back.

Gordy bent down and covered my mouth with his hand. "Shhhh."

I listened. The sounds of something crashing through the woods filled the early night sky. I carefully made my way to my feet and readied the crossbow. "Which way?" I asked in a whisper.

Vance pointed behind us and in front of us. "At least two," he whispered back.

"Let's get to the tower," Gordy said.

There was thirty feet of snow-covered ground between us and the stairs.

"I'd rather deal with this on solid ground," Vance said.

I nodded. "Agreed."

Gordy grunted. "No one ever listens to me."

"Did you ever think that might be why we're still alive," I said with my eye on the tree line in front of us.

"Ha ha," he said. He let out a gasp when he saw two Gore step out of the woods.

Squinting Vance said. "What do we got?"

"Gore," I said.

"The heads! What kind of heads?"

"Cow," I answered. "Both of them."

"They aren't bulls are they?"

I looked closer. "How am I supposed to tell?"

"Are they pissed?"

"Yeah."

"Then they're bulls," Vance said. "Damn! Bull-heads. Suckers are mean as hell."

One more stepped out of the woods behind us.

"Monkey-head behind us," Gordy said.

I turned and looked. "Chimpanzee."

Gordy rolled his eyes. "Same difference."

"A chimp-head. Almost as bad as the bull-heads," Vance said.

"Are there any nice ones?" Gordy asked

"Depends on how you define nice," Vance said gripping his pitchfork.

The two bull-heads separated, walked slowly and kept their milk-colored eyes on us.

"Nice," Gordy said, "as in they won't kill us for parts."

Vance shook his head. "Then no, there aren't any nice ones. Some are more gentle about it than others, but they all want just one thing..."

The chimp-head let out a series of hoots. The two bull-heads responded with snorts.

Minnow slowly moved toward the chimp-head with his knife drawn.

We heard a grunt overhead. Ajax and Ariabod's giant heads were peering down from the deck of the fire tower. They both disappeared and then reappeared scrambling down the steps of the tower.

The Gore were either too focused on us to notice, or they didn't care. They continued moving towards us sharing sounds back and forth. It felt like they were coordinating their attack.

A fourth Gore stepped out of the woods in front of us.

"A new one," I said.

"What kind?" Vance asked.

I groaned out, "Baby-head."

Vance gasped and shouted, "Baby-head? Cover your ears!" He frantically removed his pack and opened it. "Cover your ears!"

The baby-head Gore stood at the tree line and swayed side-to-side.

Vance pulled out a small plastic box and opened it. "Got six left," he said taking two. "Hurry, plug up your ears."

I took two and stuffed them in my ears just as the baby-head opened its mouth. It whined just as any unhappy baby would.

Gordy stood holding the ear plugs in his hands. He was staring at the baby-head Gore. Tears started to roll down his cheeks.

Vance took the plugs from him and stuffed them in Gordy's ears.

Ariabod leapt off the staircase at the midway point and landed on the back of one of the bull-heads. They both tumbled to the ground in a heap. The gorilla was ripping the patched together Gore to shreds.

Ajax reached the ground and charged the chimp-head behind us. He rumbled past Minnow and dove into the confused Gore. The gorilla warrior tore the head from the body and smashed it to the ground.

Minnow jumped on the flailing headless Gore and went for the hands.

The remaining bull-head stopped and spread out its arm. Squatting down, it let out a horrific bellow.

Vance shook his head. "Damn these eyes."

I fired an arrow and hit it in the chest.

Gordy, still crying, stood motionless staring at the baby-head gore.

Vance grabbed hold of my elbow and tucked the pitchfork under his arm. "Get me close enough so I can stab it through."

I did as he requested. The Gore stood in front of us struggling to remove the arrow I had hit it with.

Vance released my elbow and then rammed the pitchfork into the Gore's exposed ribs. It bellowed even louder than before.

"Now what?" I asked.

"Don't know! This is usually where Minnow comes in! He'd have this thing's head off by now!"

The Gore jerked and knocked Vance into me, sending us both to the ground.

It let out another squeal as Ajax came out of the darkness and pulled its feet out from under it. Before the bull-head could let out another sound, the great ape smashed its skull with his enormous fists.

I sat up and tried to catch my breath. I watched with horror and wonder as Minnow cut the chimp-head Gore to pieces. Ariabod paced on all fours in front of his dismembered Gore, and Ajax bluff charged the baby-head Gore.

"Damn," Vance said. "He didn't get the plugs in fast enough."

"What?" I said looking at him.

He motioned to something behind my left shoulder.

I turned and watched as Gordy approached the baby-head Gore in a trance. "Gordy," I said standing.

"No use," Vance said. "He's dialed in."

"Dialed in? What does that mean?"

"Baby-head over there's got your friend under its spell. If that boy had a knife, he would have already cut off one of his hands."

Ajax reached out and shoved Gordy back. Gordy stumbled, regained his footing and attempted to approach the baby-head Gore again. Ajax grabbed him by his coat and dragged him towards us.

"Gordy," I said. "Snap out of it."

"You might as well be talking to a tree. His mind is locked in on one thing. Making that baby-head happy. And there's only one thing that will make it happy. A nice brand new set of hands."

Gordy said, "My hands. My hands," with his eyes locked on the baby-head. "It needs my hands."

Ajax roared and barreled towards the Gore, but it quickly vanished into the woods.

I caught up to Gordy and grabbed his arm. "Gordy, snap out of it."

He continued to try and walk forward. Sobbing, he kept on repeating, "My hands."

Vance stood by sticking the pitchfork in the ground and pulling himself up by the handle. "Whatever you do, don't lose sight of that baby-head."

I looked through the tree line and thought I saw it moving.

"We need to catch it and kill the head." He said hobbling up next to me. "Your friend will be mentally gone until we can break the hold that thing has got on him. The only way to break the hold is to kill it. Burn the head."

I stepped in front of Gordy and made eye-to-eye contact with him, but he couldn't see me. He had no idea I was there. I pushed him back using all my strength. Nothing I did could stop him from trying to get away from me and continue towards the baby-head Gore. Finally, I called for Ariabod. The huge silverback lumbered towards us huffing and puffing. He was covered in blood and guts from the bull-head Gore. "Hold him back," I said handing Gordy's arm to the gorilla. "Sit on him if you have to. Just don't let him loose."

Ariabod grinned and nodded his pointy head.

Minnow approached covered in his own share of blood and guts. He wiped a chunk of something from his cheek still holding his knife.

"Take Minnow with you," Vance said.

I hesitated.

"Take my word for it. The boy can hunt down a Gore in a blinding snow storm with zero visibility."

I nodded.

Vance packed some snow in a ball and tossed it in the boy's direction. It missed by a mile, but still managed to get his attention. Minnow ran through icy snow towards the mangled man. "Go with Oz," Vance said with exaggerated mouth movements. "Help him find that baby-head."

The boy stared at Vance.

"With Oz," Vance said pointing to me. "Find baby-head."

Ajax rumbled forward and stared at the boy before sitting on his haunches. He reeled off a series of signs.

The boy watched him intently. A smile spread across his face just as a tear fell from his left eye. He signed back to Ajax, his grin growing bigger.

Ajax grunted and nodded his head.

Minnow raced toward the woods.

"Where's he going?" I asked. "Wait!"

"He can't hear you," Vance said. He focused his attention on Ajax. "Heard a lot about you, Mr. Ajax."

I ran after the boy.

Vance whistled.

I turned back to him, and he tossed me the pitchfork. "You're going to need that. Trust me."

I sprinted toward the woods.

Wes and Tyrone reached the bottom of the stairs.

"Get everybody up top," I said as I entered the woods still trying to catch up to Minnow.

"What in the hell is going on?" Wes asked.

"Ask Vance!"

"Who the hell is Vance?"

I didn't bother answering his question. I pushed my way through the low hanging, ice-covered limbs. Minnow was having an easier time of traveling through the dense brush than I was, but somehow I managed to catch up to him. I placed my hand on his shoulder.

He spun around with his knife drawn and a look that said he was just a breath away from cutting me to pieces.

"Whoa! Whoa! Whoa! Slow down."

He bared his teeth.

"You've got a good idea what we're getting into, but I'm just putting things together…"

His eyes shifted to above my head, and he tightened his grip on his knife. I saw a shadow move across his face.

"It's behind me, isn't it?"

He didn't respond. He just kept his eyes locked on the space above me.

I took a deep breath and whirled around. The baby-head Gore towered over me. Its body was a disgusting mix of flesh and bones from more animals than I could count. Its hands were human. The right hand was a child's, but the left appeared to be an adult male. I scanned up the body and nearly vomited at the sight of the baby's face looking back at me. The skin was peeling from the forehead and one ear dangled, attached only at the earlobe. I could hear muffled whimpering. It was a pathetic sight. I even felt sorry for it.

Minnow rushed around me and dove at the Gore. The monster seemed terrified by the small boy. It stepped back and bawled like a frightened baby.

"Stop," I said. "You're scaring it."

Minnow couldn't hear me. He rammed the knife into the fur-covered belly and then slashed away at the legs.

"Stop," I said backing away. I don't know why I wanted him to stop. I knew it was a monster. I knew it wanted to kill us, but it was so sad. I could feel how sad it was.

The Gore fell to one knee and then the other. It's baby face pouted, and it whined.

"You're hurting it."

Minnow stopped long enough to give me a quick glance. He shook his head in disgust and then walked behind the creature and rammed the knife through its neck. The baby-head cried louder. With a quick twist, the head fell to the ground, landing face first in the snow.

I fell to the ground and sobbed. I couldn't understand why. It was a freakish monster. It wanted my hands. It would have killed me. I was sure of it, but I still couldn't help feeling horribly sad for it. It was so, so scared.

Minnow picked the head up and exited the woods. I remained on the ground trying to figure out what had just happened. I did nothing while a small deaf boy butchered a grotesque creature with a baby's head. It didn't just have a baby's head. It acted like a baby. It cried and whined like a baby. It pouted like a baby. It felt to me as if Minnow had just murdered a poor innocent baby.

And I did nothing.

Chapter Nine

We sat in a circle in the cabin of the fire tower staring at the head. Introductions had been made, and we were all catching our breaths, trying to sort out in our minds what had just happened. Everyone but Minnow. He stared in awe at Ajax.

"So, what in the hell are we dealing with here?" Wes asked.

"Gore," Vance said.

"I can see that. It's Gory as hell."

"No," Vance said. "They're called Gore, as in the Gore. That fella Floyd knew all about them."

"Floyd? You know Floyd the cook?"

Vance nodded. "Wish like hell I didn't, but I do."

Wes gave me a 'See, I told you so,' grin.

"The Gore are people. That is to say, they walk like people. Some of them talk like people…"

Wes chuckled. "From what I saw, they don't much look like people."

"No they don't," Vance said. "They put themselves together with whatever parts they can find from whatever animal or human they can find. You do not want to be around when they need to replace a part."

"Wait, so if they walk and talk like people, do they think... like people?"

Vance shook his head. "Not as far as I can tell. They organize and work together. And when they talk, it's only the human heads, and it's mostly nonsense that comes out of their mouths. Kind of like they're repeating old conversations they had when they were alive. Floyd talked about a couple that could think and talk intelligently, but I've never come across one."

Gordy was staring holes in the baby head.

"Is he going to be okay?" I asked.

"In time," Vance said. "The baby-heads are the worst ones. They don't attack or come at you. They lure you in. Make you sad for them. Once you hear them crying, you're under their spell. The earplugs help, but you get close enough they can still get through to you."

"Yeah," I said. "I felt it."

He pointed to Minnow. "That's why I sent the boy with you. Kid's deaf as a…" You could practically see the gears turning in his head. "What the hell kind of animal is deaf?" He thought some more and then said, "Whatever. The kid's deaf."

I looked at Minnow. "He's got skills."

"Pissed all to hell is his skill. The Gore got his parents. Kid didn't shed a tear. Something flipped inside of him. He's been a pint-sized super ninja ever since."

The baby-head's eyes opened startling us all.

I quickly put my fingers in my ears.

"No need," Vance said leaning in and squinting. "Head can't hurt you. Only works when there're more parts plugged into it."

"How come the gorillas aren't under its spell? They didn't have earplugs."

"Best I can figure," Vance said, "is that it gives off different frequencies for whatever animal is around. That thing saw a bunch of humans with perfectly good hands, and it set itself to our frequency, not the apes."

"What are we going to do with this thing?" Tyrone asked, scooting as far away from it as he could.

Vance pointed to the wood-burning stove. "Burn it. The sooner the better. The body's probably wandering around below looking for it... or a replacement head."

Wes moved to the stove and stoked the embers. He threw some paper in to ignite the flames. A pile of kindling lay near the wall. He stuffed a few pieces in and flames popped out of the open door.

"Fire's not hot enough to burn something like that," Tyrone said. "We talked about that before. It has to be hot, hot. Like 1800 degrees hot."

Vance shook his head. "We're not trying to cremate it. The flames just take the life out of it. I don't know why, but it works."

"Bring it here," Wes said.

"I'm not touching it," Tyrone said.

I got on my knees and took a deep breath. The head's eyes focused on me. I placed both hands over its ears and lifted it off the ground. It giggled, and I nearly dropped it.

"All tricks, son," Vance said. "It's nothing but a head with a monster inside it playing you like a fiddle."

I hurried to the stove and shoved the head inside. Wes quickly shut the door, and we both backed away, horrified that it was screaming. In unison, we turned to Vance. He mimicked playing a fiddle.

Gordy cleared his throat and said, "I'm hungry." He then sniffed the air. "What smells so good?"

Chapter Ten

I stood on the deck alone and watched two headless Gore stagger in the snow below us. They were searching for their heads or new ones in the darkness. If wasn't so terrifying it would have been funny.

A brisk wind blew falling snow into my face. I shielded my eyes, and something underneath a thin layer of ice on the railing caught my attention. I chipped away at it and noticed my name carved in the wood. I quickly cleared away more of the ice. I could make out the words, "be with." I chipped away all the ice and read the message out loud. "I will always be with Oz." It was the first physical evidence that Lou was here.

I read it out loud and heard the words float away on the thin cold wind. I said it over and over again. Each time the words left my mouth the angrier I got. She wasn't with me. She left me. She snuck away into the cold and abandoned me. She didn't just leave me. She left all of us. I hated her for it. I hated her. I hated her. I hated her.

I didn't really. I knew it as soon as the thought entered my head. I loved her, and I think that's why I felt so much hatred for her. It was confusing. No one had taught me about these things. I grew up in a world where killing monsters was the only skill that mattered. Hating things was a way of life.

Being in love was new to me. Being without the one I loved was torture. Torture I was used to. Torture was something I could deal with. Love wasn't. And maybe that's just the way Stevie wanted it. Maybe this was all part of his plan, too. Maybe that's why he created Lou. She wasn't here to help me at all. She was here to destroy me.

Wes approached from the other side of the deck and looked at me for a long time before speaking. "You got a thinking face on, boy."

I didn't answer. I continued to watch the headless Gore.

"Ugly cusses, ain't they?" Wes said.

I nodded.

"Pretty nippy to be out here spying on a couple of headless goons."

"I guess," I said.

"You gonna tell me what's on your mind, or am I going to have to guess."

I shrugged and covered up Lou's message with my arm. "I was just wondering what our next move should be."

Wes propped himself against the railing and it creaked from supporting his weight. "Well, what do you think about backtracking?"

"Backtracking?"

"To where we met up with that Floyd fella. It's pretty clear that he was the last to see Lou. Hell, he may still be traveling with her. I figure if we go back to where we last saw him we just might be able to pick up his trail."

"We'd be losing a day," I said. "Maybe more if the weather gets worse."

He agreed. "It is the wrong direction, and it may not get us any closer to Lou."

"Nothing will get you closer to your Lou," Vance said. Wes and I turned to see him standing just past the doorway to the cabin.

"What do you mean by that?" Wes asked.

He limped towards us. "Your Lou is gone."

I felt ill. My face started to burn in the freezing cold. "Gone?"

He made his way to the railing and looked over. "Gone. In the head. Looney tunes."

A wave of relief came over me.

"You don't know Lou," Wes said. "If she's gone crazy like you say, she won't stay that way."

"Well, I have no doubt the girl you knew was full of pluck and good sense…"

"The girl we know," Wes said cutting him off, "is a fierce warrior that's beat down the meanest beasties you can imagine. She'll be fine. More than fine."

Vance shook his head. "She's got a long road ahead of her to get back to fine." He held up his handless arm. "Your fierce warrior did this to me."

I fumbled with the thoughts racing through my head. He had to be wrong or lying. Lou didn't cut off his hand.

"Don't get me wrong. I was glad she did it. I asked her to do it. I begged her to do it."

Wes and I looked at him confused.

"Or course, she wouldn't do it unless I promised to help her cut her hand off."

The words barely reached my ears before I grabbed him by his collar and pushed him back.

"I didn't do it," he said trying to keep his balance.

Wes pulled me back. "You better get on with your story before I let the boy lay into you."

"It's the Gore. She got dialed into a baby-head. Me, too. The Gore crave hands more than anything else. They can't get enough of them. Hands, hands, hands." He examined his remaining hand. "It's a pretty remarkable appendage if you think about it." He flexed his fingers. "Can't blame them really."

"Get on with it," Wes said.

Vance cleared his throat. "My baby-head asked for my hands. When it asked, it made perfect sense to me. I couldn't understand how I hadn't given it my hands earlier. I was an idiot for not thinking of it myself. It was as if the poor thing was a guest in my house, and I hadn't offered it a glass of water. It was just that obvious."

Wes raised an eyebrow. "Now, you'll have to excuse me for saying so, but I think you may be the crazy one."

Vance smiled. "You're right. At least I was crazy. Lou and I were crazy together. That's why she helped me cut off my hand. She understood. She knew how I felt. We made a pact. She would help me cut off my hands for the Gore, and I would help her cut off hers for the Gore."

I looked at him suspiciously. "You just said 'hands," as in both of them. Why did you stop at one?"

He motioned with his head towards the cabin. "Minnow is the reason I still have one hand." He chuckled. "You probably don't know this, but having your hand cut off while you're awake and fully aware hurts like a mother. Don't get me wrong. I was glad to do it. Cried tears of joy the entire time your Lou was sawing through my wrist. But, thankfully, I was too drained to have her cut off the other one right away. I needed to rest. That's when Minnow caught on to what we were doing. He did the only thing he knows how to do."

"Which is?" Wes asked.

"Sliced my baby-head Gore to pieces. Burned it. All of it. Released me from its hold. All the crazy went away. Too late to save one of my hands, but I got to keep the other one, and this backwards world is down a Gore."

"So if killing your Gore released you, why won't killing Lou's release her?"

"It will, but her Gore's long gone. It didn't want her hands. It couldn't use them. Don't know why, but it just up and left. Broke Lou's heart. Minnow and I tried to help her, but she wouldn't have any of it. Her mind is fixed on giving her hands to her Gore." He paused and stared off into space. "Can you imagine wanting to sacrifice yourself for something only to find out your sacrifice isn't wanted? Hell, it's more than that. Her sacrifice isn't even considered worthy."

I stepped back and returned to watching the headless Gore below. Lou's carved message caught my eye. "We shouldn't backtrack."

Wes groaned. "But Lou…"

"She's headed to Buffalo. Crazy or not, that's' where she's headed. The sooner we get there, the sooner we find her."

"I told you, kid," Vance said, "North isn't the way you want to go. You want to go anywhere but north. The Gore are gathering up north."

"I see," Wes said. "And just how do you know this?"

"The same way I know everything about the Gore. Floyd told me."

"Floyd?" Wes said with a laugh.

"The guy's a straight up shithead, but he knows the Gore. Better than Minnow. Minnow hates the big ugly piles of crap. Floyd loves them."

"Loves them?" I asked with disbelief.

"Like he was one of them. He serves them. Does whatever he can to keep them happy."

Wes scratched his chin. "He wasn't missing any body parts when we saw him."

Vance shook his head. "He doesn't have to give them his hands. He is their hands. His whole life is about getting them whatever they need." He started to limp away but stopped. "Even if what they need is a leg from the guy who gave him food and shelter in a blizzard." With that he winked and walked back into the cabin.

Chapter Eleven

I wasn't the first one to wake the next morning. Minnow was sitting on the floor watching Ajax sleep. He didn't even notice me as I moved about the room gathering up my supplies. After my pack was full, I approached him from behind and watched him watching the sleeping gorilla.

My foot slid across the wooden floor when I shifted my weight to my left leg. Ajax huffed and peeked past his arm that covered his huge head. He let out a little muffled bark when he saw Minnow's smiling face peering down at him. He leaned forward and shifted his eyes from the kid to me.

"Talk to him," I said. "The kid thinks you're some kind of god or something."

Ajax rolled on his stomach and pushed himself up on his hands and then sat back on his haunches. He frowned at Minnow and then signed to the boy.

Minnow excitedly signed back.

I didn't remember most of the signs I had learned before, but I swear it looked like the kid was calling Ajax "sir." The thought of it made me laugh. Ajax growled at me and continued to sign.

Tyrone was the next to wake up. He stood and stretched and then joined me in watching the boy and the gorilla signing together. "What are they talking about?" he asked.

I shrugged. "I've caught a few words. Something about stories. The kid reads a lot is about all I'm getting out of the conversation."

"I thought you knew how to talk with your hands like that."

I shook my head. "Lou does. Not me. I know a word or letter here and there, but…" I stopped when I noticed a familiar sign. "The kid just said Buffalo."

I leaned in closer. Ajax and Minnow were signing back and forth at a frenzied pace. I made out a few more words: war, doctor, die, and Creyshaw. I asked Ajax a number of times to slow down so I could try and make out a few more words. He tried to do as I asked, but he only managed to slow it down for a few words before he was back to hurriedly signing.

I woke up Vance.

"What is wrong with you? Sleep is as precious as gold around here. You don't ever wake a man in a deep sleep."

I pointed to Ajax and Minnow. "I want to know what they're saying."

Vance looked at them and sat up. "You know what they're saying. They're saying don't ever wake a man when he's asleep."

"Seriously," I said. "What are they saying?"

Vance grumbled. "I haven't the first clue. I don't know that sign language stuff."

"Nothing?"

"Not a word."

"How have you been communicating with the kid?"

"What communicating? I just mouth 'kill' and the boy's raring to go."

I sighed and sat down, watching the conversation in sign language go on, feeling more and more frustrated I couldn't understand what they were saying.

Vance attached his rifle-butt leg and stretched. "Start the coffee yet?"

"Coffee?"

His expression turned to horror. "Don't tell me you don't have coffee."

I didn't say anything.

He grimaced. "I will put up with a lot of things. Tell me California fell into the ocean, and I wouldn't give a flip. Poke out my eyes and feed them to zombie squirrels, and it wouldn't bother me a bit. Sock me in the stomach as hard as you can, and I will let it slide. But try and tell me you do not have coffee, and I will lose my ever-loving mind."

Wes sat up and yawned. "Coffee? I haven't seen a cup of joe in…I don't know how long."

"So there's really no coffee?"

I slowly shook my head and tried to conceal a smile

Vance stood and dressed quickly.

"Where you going?" Wes asked.

"To get us some coffee." He looked around for his hat and gloves.

"You going back to the lodge?" I asked.

He shook his head. "Got enough for one measly little cup back there. Today's my restocking day anyway. Might as well get to it."

Gordy quickly sat up. "Restocking? Is this the same place where you got the chocolate?"

Vance nodded. "Chocolate, MREs, soda, Twinkies…"

"Twinkies?" Wes said excitedly.

"Shelves and shelves of Twinkies," Vance said.

Wes clapped his hands and howled. "Hot dog! I'm going with you!"

Gordy stood up. "I'm going, too."

"Hold on," I said.

"Don't see why not," Vance said. "You folks are interested in heading north anyhow, and this place is in that direction. You can stock up and be on your way."

I tried not to appear shocked. "You'd share your supplies with us."

He laughed. "Kid, I could live twenty lifetimes and not eat everything this place has. Besides, it's not my stock. It belonged to someone else. I just found it."

"That settles it then," Wes said gathering his stuff. "Let's get on with it and get to them Twinkies."

We all went about preparing to leave. We were actually almost upbeat.

Gordy rolled up his sleeping bag and then asked Vance, "Are there zombie squirrels around here?"

Vance stopped gave the question some thought and then busted out laughing.

Chapter Twelve

We were back in the tunnels within the hour. Vance led the way, and Ariabod brought up the rear. The rest of us lit the way with glow sticks in one hand while we held various weapons in the other hand. The tunnel went on for what seemed like miles. Every 300 yards or so we would enter a small chamber that split off into two, sometimes three, different directions. Minnow had painted different colored arrows on the walls.

"You see the red arrows? They will take us to the warehouse," he said. "The boy used to use them to help him find the way. They don't do me a lick of good. Thank goodness for smells and drafts. The boy doesn't even need the arrows now."

"Warehouse?" Wes asked.

"That's what I call it. It's a huge underground room. I swear you could park a jetliner in it. Place is packed with every survival supply you can think of."

"And you have no idea who built it?" I asked.

"Nope, but I figure it was the government or military or something. Took a lot of clams, I know that."

"Clams?" Gordy asked.

Vance huffed out a laugh. "Money. moo-la, deniros... mucho dinero "

We reached yet another small room, and Vance suggested we rest. "Got another forty minutes or so of walking. We should take some time to power up."

We all found spots on the concrete floor to sit and munch on some granola.

"What were you before?" Wes asked Vance as he dug into his bag of granola.

"Before?"

"Your job."

"Sales. Custom windows. Crap job. You?"

"Mechanic. Best job ever."

Vance nodded. "I get that. Working with your hands, figuring stuff out. I sat at a desk 90% of the time calling leads that filled out forms to win a free jet ski. Crap job."

"You said that," Wes said.

"Can't say it enough." He yawned. "I need coffee."

"Ain't you going to ask what we did?" Gordy asked.

Vance grinned. "What were you, doctors and lawyers?"

"Football player," Gordy said.

"You were?" I said sounding surprised.

He shrugged. "I was gonna be. We both were."

"We were?" I said sounding just as surprised as before.

"We talked about it."

"We talked about playing for the Titans. The NFL. It was just kid stuff."

"To you maybe. I could've done it. Never got the chance."

He couldn't have. Gordy was slow and couldn't walk without tripping over his own feet, but I didn't really see the point in telling him he would have never played in the NFL.

"You know what I wanted to be when I was a kid?" Vance asked no one in particular. "I wanted to be a writer."

Gordy rolled his eyes. "What? Like books and stuff?"

"Yeah, books and stuff. Don't tell me you don't like to read."

"Read? What for? There're movies and games and stuff…" he stopped when he realized he was wrong.

"You see," Vance said with a smirk. "All that time you spent playing video games and watching movies, and where are they now?" He stuck his tongue out and squeaked out a raspberry as he gave us a thumbs down. "Gone, gone, gone. But books? They are all over the place just waiting to be picked up and read. Books don't care that the world is over. We aren't the only living things to survive. Books are just as alive as us. More alive than us."

"You're crazy," Gordy said dismissively.

Vance reached in his backpack and pulled out a book. Holding it up, he said, "Picked this up in a house somewhere a while back. Can't read it anymore. Not since my glasses broke, but when I could, man, it wasn't snowing outside. There weren't those Gore running around. I wasn't hungry or tired and depressed all to hell. I was in this book. This living, breathing book." He tossed it to Gordy. "Take it."

"Me? Why?"

"Because that book's calling for you."

Gordy examined it. He ran his hand across the torn cover and then flipped through the pages. "I don't hear anything."

"You start reading it and you will." Vance turned his attention to Tyrone. "What about you, young fella?"

Tyrone didn't look his way. "What about me?"

"What were you before all this started?"

"He was a little kid, a little, little kid," I said.

"No, I wasn't," Tyrone said. "I mean that's not all I was."

We waited for Tyrone to finish his thought, but he just continued to dig through his bag of granola.

"Well?" Vance asked.

Tyrone looked at him. "Well, what?"

"What were you if weren't just a kid?"

Tyrone thought about his question. He dropped his eyes to the concrete floor and said, "I was my grandfather's grandson. That's what I was."

Vance cleared his throat. "Still are."

Tyrone shook his head. "Nah. Stopped being that a long time ago. The things I do here. The way I live. I'm not that kid anymore. I'm not his grandson." He pointed up. "I'm like those things up there, a brainless monster looking for whatever I can to keep me alive, and most of the time I gotta kill things to get that stuff. And I don't really care. My grandfather cared about things. I cared about things. I don't now." He stuck his granola back in his pack and stood up. "I say we get going."

Vance wasn't eager to agree with Tyrone about ending our break, but he gave in after hemming and hawing over his throbbing nub of a leg. I stood and helped him up and offered to carry his supplies, but he wouldn't have any of it.

"The second I give into the limitations of a one-legged man is the second I'll become a one-legged man."

Gordy got out the word, "But…" before I cut him off. He was going tell Vance he was a one-legged man. I didn't see the use in it.

We continued down a new corridor and broke out the last few glow sticks we had. The clank-clank sound of Vance's rifle butt leg was the only sound that was made the rest of the trip. When that sound stopped, Vance spoke the first words any of us had said in thirty minutes. "We're here."

"We are?" Gordy said sticking his neck out trying to get a better view. "I don't see anything."

In point of fact, Gordy was right. There was nothing to see. 'Here' appeared to be a dead-end. The only thing in front of us was a cinder block wall.

"It's here. Trust me," Vance said.

There was a brief moment of confused silence before Wes said, "This is your warehouse?"

Vance groaned. "No, this isn't it. This is how we get in."

"How we get in?" I asked.

Vance cleared his throat. "Okay, this is going to seem weird, but hear me out. Close your eyes and say, 'Open sesame.'"

Wes, Gordy, Tyrone, and I shared a confused expression.

"C'mon," Vance said. "Hurry up. I want to get to my coffee."

One-by-one, we all closed our eyes.

Vance said, "Say the words."

Wes started, and we all quickly joined in.

When we finished, Vance giggled. "You're a gullible bunch."

We opened our eyes.

He pushed a cinder block in front of him, and the entire wall slowly started to tilt back. In a matter of seconds, the wall became a ramp that led down to a polished concrete floor. Wes and I poked our heads past the opening and peeked inside. A slight hum came out of nowhere followed by a series of clicks as light after light turned on and lit up the enormous space.

Rows of shelves full of various supplies stretched out as far as we could see. I stepped past the opening, craned my neck back and nearly gasped when I saw how high the shelves were. They must have been thirty feet high. The space appeared to be as wide as it was long.

Minnow hurried past us and disappeared behind a row of shelves to our left while Vance headed right towards a room in the corner of the warehouse. He whistled, and the tune echoed throughout the space.

"Holy crap," Gordy said. "This is... it's beautiful."

Wes smiled and slapped him on the back. "I couldn't have said it better, boy."

The light went on in the room Vance entered. I walked toward him and watched through a large window as he prepared a coffee maker. The others hooted and roared with laughter as they darted from aisle to aisle. The gorillas were even joining in the fun.

I reached the doorway to the room, and watched Vance for a few minutes before I said, "I don't understand how this place can be."

"Neither do I, kid. Neither do I." He pushed the brewing button on the coffee maker.

"There's electricity, running water, food…"

"I know. Isn't it great?" He said holding a coffee cup, anxiously waiting for the coffee to finish brewing.

"It's a little too great," I said.

"Too great?" He looked at me like I was an idiot. "Kid, you have to get this notion out of your head that just because the world ended there aren't any good surprises left to find."

I didn't answer. "It just doesn't add up."

"No, it doesn't, but it doesn't really matter to me how you add it up because it sure as hell comes out in our favor."

I shook my head.

"Alright, you want a plausible explanation for all this?"

"I'd be happy if you could just explain one thing."

He smiled. "I can do that. Give me the one thing you want explained."

"How is there electricity?"

Clearly stumped, he opened his mouth but then quickly closed it when he realized he didn't have a complete thought on the matter. Finally, he snapped his fingers and said, "Solar power."

"Solar power? Underground?"

"No, the panels aren't underground. You remember I used to sell custom windows. Well, we had a solar power division in the company. I knew this nut job that built a bomb shelter in his back yard. It was underground like this, and he had us put a crap load of solar panels topside to provide it with electricity."

I thought about his explanation. "Solar panels, huh?"

He nodded with a smile and then quickly turned to the coffee maker to fill his cup.

"There's something else I need you to explain," I said.

He poured sugar in his coffee. "Go right ahead. I'm Mr. Answer-man today."

"Why would you ever leave this place?"

He stirred his coffee. "Well, if it was up to me I wouldn't."

"Who else would it be up to?"

Vance motioned with his head toward the warehouse. "The little ninja."

I saw Minnow running up an aisle with a box of Cheerios.

"The little guy has got a score to settle, and I ain't got it in me to let him do it alone. I'd be lying if I didn't admit I get a great deal of satisfaction killing Gore, but the kid, well he lives for it. It's the reason he gets up in the morning. If he didn't have Gore to kill, I'm afraid to think what would become of him."

I watched Minnow for a few more seconds and then turned to see Vance's eyes roll back in his head as he sipped from his coffee.

"Good Lord!" he shouted. "Good Lord! Good Lord! Good Lord!" He took another sip and then let out a gleeful sigh.

I looked around the warehouse and suddenly was struck by an idea. "This place have books?"

Vance nodded before drinking from his cup. When he had taken in as much coffee as he could, he swallowed and said, "Tons." He pointed to the right. "The far end aisle. Go all the way to the other side of the warehouse. There are rows and rows of books there. There's a computer that will tell you where to find most any book you want."

I left him to his cup of coffee and headed to the last aisle. The enormity of the place was hard to believe. As I entered the aisle, I marveled at the sheer volume of supplies on either side of me. Anything you could think of to not just survive, but to thrive, was in this place. I took a mental note of the items I passed so I could come back and pick through the shelves. It felt like it was Christmas morning and I found a stack of presents under the tree.

After a long walk, I reached the shelves that housed thousands of books. It was almost overwhelming. I strolled from shelf to shelf and glanced at the spines. They seemed to be organized as they would have been in a library. As I rounded a corner to start down another aisle, I spotted the computer Vance had told me about. I tapped in the words 'sign language' and waited as the computer screen assured me it was searching. In short order, a list of books popped up on the screen. I ran my finger down the list and stopped when I found one that was titled 'American Sign Language for Children.' It sounded like it was just my speed.

I repeated the catalog and shelf number to myself over and over again as I zigzagged my way through the aisle. When I found the book, I flipped through some pages and was happy to see it was easy enough for even me to follow.

I emerged from the aisle with my head down, examining some of the illustrations when I heard a loud whistle and hoot. The sound echoed throughout the cavernous space. I bolted down the larger aisle, feeling less panicked as I heard the sound of laughter.

I was almost out of breath by the time I reached the other end of the building. I stopped and took a few minutes to catch my breath, scanning the area for the source of the sound. Wes was standing at the far wall, huddled over a table reading something. I saw his shoulders shake as he let out another laugh.

"Wes!" I shouted.

Still focused on whatever he was reading he said, "You're not going to believe this."

I allowed myself a second or two more of rest and then hurried to his side. He was looking down at a blueprint. I didn't have a lot of experience reading blueprints, but I guessed it was the warehouse. He pulled it back and revealed a second set of blueprints.

"You know what this is?" he asked.

I leaned down and scanned the complex drawing. I could only identify one image. Pointing, I asked, "Are those railroad tracks?"

He nodded. "Yep. The best I can figure is this is a schematic of a railroad station."

I looked at the blueprint one more time and prepared to walk away. "That's nice, Wes."

"Hold up," he said. "It's not so much a railroad station as it is a subway station."

"Subway?"

"Yeah, like they got in the big cities up north."

"Underground?"

"That is what subway means."

"Must be some kind of historical document," I said.

He shook his head and showed me the first set of blueprints again. "You see these numbers at the top here?" he asked, pointing. "Those are GPS coordinates. That's this underground warehouse where we're standing right now."

"Okay?"

He showed me the second set of blueprints and pointed to the same numbers at the top of the page, except the word 'Sub-Level" was written next to them. "Same numbers. And what do you reckon sub-level means?"

I thought about it and then looked down at my feet. "Below us?"

"That's right. There's a subway station below us. I'd bet money on it." He reached across the table and grabbed a half-eaten Twinkie.

"How could that be? I mean that's not possible. A subway station in the middle of nowhere?"

He chuckled with a mouthful of Twinkie. "Not possible? Have you forgotten where you are?"

I took the first set of blueprints from him and examined it. "Okay, how do we get down there?" I still wasn't completely buying it, but I had to admit stranger things had happened.

He grabbed another Twinkie and unwrapped it. Looking over my shoulder, he said, "For some fool reason they've left the entrance off the blueprints. It's like they were trying to hide it."

"Who's 'they'?"

He shrugged. "They... The people who built this place."

"If you're right, they didn't just build this place. They built a whole subway system, right?"

He nodded while biting off a chunk of Twinkie. "That's what I'm thinking. No telling where it goes. Smart as hell if you think about it. You could sneak around wherever you wanted with a whole entire underground railroad. Had to be the government. Why else do you reckon you have to have a permit to dig a hole? They didn't want no one digging into their subway. This is why I never trusted our government..."

"Whoa," I said, "let's not get ahead of ourselves. We should probably find the place first and then discuss your crazy conspiracy theories."

"Crazy? That word don't mean much around here." He stepped back from the table and looked around. "Now, we just gotta think our way around this."

I stepped back and searched the walls for a door.

"Let's say west is in front of where we're standing. If you were to lay the blueprints over one another, lining up the GPS coordinates, that's where the tracks we would be. Logic tells us they ain't gonna build an entrance down to the tracks themselves." He wheeled around. "That means the entrance is probably near the east side of this room."

I followed him as he slowly walked toward the other side of the warehouse. Vance stepped out of the small room holding onto a fresh cup of coffee. The steam rose out of the cup and then whipped suddenly towards the wall behind him.

"What's got into you two?" He asked, taking a sip from his cup with the steam rushing around his head.

Wes stopped and watched him drink.

"What?" I asked, trying not to run into him.

Vance lowered his cup. "What are you staring at?"

Wes reached for me and then pointed at Vance. "See the steam coming off that cup?"

"Yeah, so?"

"Something's got a hold of it... a draft."

I still didn't get what he was trying to say.

"Where there's a draft," he said walking at a quick pace toward Vance. "There's usually a door."

"He's standing in a doorway," I said following him.

"The steams moving away from it," he said, "Towards that back corner."

Vance watched as we passed him and placed our hands on the concrete wall. "You two have gone spinners on me."

Wes gently knocked on the hard surface.

"Nobody's home," Vance said with a cuckle.

I moved around Wes and stood in the corner. I didn't see anything close to resembling a door. I did a half turn to let Wes know I thought it was a dead end when I stopped. Something caught my attention. It almost felt like a…

"What?" Wes asked.

I didn't answer right away. I couldn't be sure if I actually felt anything at all. Several seconds passed, and I was about to tell him that it was nothing, when I felt it again. "A breeze."

"Where?" he asked excitedly.

I waited to feel it again. It hit my right cheek, and I pointed in the direction I thought it was coming from.

Wes moved in slowly and waited. When he thought enough time had passed, he said, "I don't feel anything…" He stopped short. "Wait, wait, wait." He stepped up and placed his ear to the wall. After a few seconds, he smiled. "It's hollow."

"Hollow?" Vance said. "That thing's solid as a rock."

Wes searched the immediate area. "There has to be a button or control panel or something. This is it. This is the door to the subway."

"Subway?" Vance asked almost spitting out his swallow of coffee. "What subway?"

"The one below us," Wes said.

Vance grinned. "You do know we're in the middle of nowhere, right? What in God's name would a subway be doing out here?"

"What would a giant underground warehouse full of food be doing out here?" Wes asked. He watched as Vance shook his head and went back into his room. Wes snapped his fingers and followed after him.

"Where are you going?"

"It's in here," Wes said. "This room... It's a..." He stood in the doorway and moved his head side to side as he searched for what he was looking for. Spotting it, he yelled, "Control room!"

I walked up behind him as he dashed to a desk at the back of the room. He pulled a canvas cover off of it and giggled madly.

Vance and I joined him.

"Good corn niblets," Vance said sounding surprised.

Before us on the desk was a series of buttons and gauges.

"What is it?" I asked.

Wes reached down and touched a few of the buttons. "It's a control panel."

Vance was confused. "But the panel for the warehouse is over there," he said pointing to the corner behind us.

"It's not for the warehouse," Wes said pointing to a small sign at the top of a row of buttons.

'Sub-Level Auxiliary Control Panel.'

Wes's eyes moved from button to button until he found what he was looking for. "W-L-E," he said.

"What's that mean?" Vance asked.

"Warehouse Level Entrance."

We all stared at the button.

Finally, Vance said, "Well, what are you waiting for? Push it!"

Wes took a deep breath, held it for a brief second and then let it out. After popping his knuckles, he pushed the button.

A couple of seconds passed, and nothing happened. Then we all jumped slightly when we heard a clanging sound from the wall. That was followed by the sound of gears turning. Wes rushed passed us, nearly knocking Vance to the ground, and exited the room.

"I was right!" we heard him shout. "It's a door! It's a door!"

Vance and I made our way out of the room and found Wes standing in front of an open doorway craning his neck to see what was inside.

"What is it?" Gordy asked, coming up from the nearest aisle.

Tyrone and the two gorillas approached from the other side of the warehouse.

Wes clapped his hands together and let out a rebel yell.

"It's a door," I said. "To a subway."

"Well," Vance said, "hold on. It's a door. I'll grant you that. Whether it leads to a subway or not, we don't know."

Wes turned to us with a big smile. "It does."

"How can you know something like that?"

His smile grew bigger, and he pointed to something past the door.

Vance and I moved forward and peered inside. I laughed when I saw what Wes was pointing to.

"What?" Vance asked. "I can't see a dang thing."

"It's a sign," I said.

"What's it say?"

I nodded at Wes. "Tell him what it says Wes."

"With pleasure," Wes said with a smile. "Train schedules are available at the information kiosk near the men's restroom."

Chapter Thirteen

Before we ventured down the stairs, we collected gear from the warehouse. In twenty minutes, we had dozens of glow sticks, new hunting knifes, two more crossbows, and three quivers full of arrows. Wes even found a half-dozen two-way radios.

Handing one to Gordy he said, "Take this. It's fully charged."

Gordy took it and switched it on. He clicked the button. "Cool."

"You're staying up top."

Gordy looked uneasy. "Up top? Here? By myself?"

Wes nodded. "You'll be safe. We're the ones going down into an abandoned subway system."

"But those things... the Gore... I mean can they get in this place?"

Vance patted him on the back. "Don't worry. That almost never happens."

Gordy tried to hand the radio back to Wes. "I'm not staying up here by myself. Take it."

"Minnow will stay with you," I said.

"What?" Vance asked with a worried expression on his face.

"He's the Gore killer, right? He should stay here and make sure they don't get in."

Vance nodded. "Yeah, but... I mean I can't just leave him here... You know, with him," he said motioning with his head toward Gordy.

"The kid?' You're leaving me with the kid?" Gordy said.

"Gordy," I said with a groan. "That kid can slice and dice a Gore better than all of us. I'm doing you a favor."

Gordy thought about it and said, "Okay, I'll watch the kid. He can stay with me."

"Ajax," I said, "tell Minnow he and Gordy are staying here in the warehouse."

Ajax knuckled walked to Minnow and quickly signed the little ninja his orders. I could tell by the scowl on his face the kid wasn't happy about it. Ajax gave him a few more signs. Minnow hesitated and then giggled. Ajax gave him a broad grin and knuckle-walked towards the door to the subway.

I wished more than ever that I remembered sign language because I was dying to know what Ajax told him to make him laugh.

With the gorillas leading the way, we descended the staircase. Remarkably, we didn't need the glow sticks. Whatever was providing electricity for the warehouse was apparently doing the same for the subway.

At the bottom of the stairs was a locked steel door. We humans scanned every nook and cranny searching for a device that would release the locks. The gorillas watched us for a good bit until they got tired of waiting. They stormed the door with their shoulders and fists, and in short order, the hinges gave way to their brute strength. Eventually enough space was left between the frame and door to allow even Wes to squeeze through.

We stood on an enormous platform. Twelve foot pillars stretched from floor to ceiling. The platform itself was about twenty feet wide, and at the end of it was a drop off down to the tracks below.

"I'll be," Wes said. "I expected to find it, but I still don't believe it."

Tyrone leaned over the platform and examined the tracks. "I see tracks but no train."

I walked to the information kiosk and looked at the map and schedule. The map was titled 'United States Eastern Sub Transport Line.' Every state from Ohio to the Atlantic Ocean and from Canada to Florida was on the map. A twisting maze of tracks snaked throughout the entire map.

"Holy moly," Wes said coming up behind me.

Vance joined us and squinted. "What's it say?"

"It says our government was keeping a big secret from us," Wes said.

"Tell me something I don't know," Vance said with a snort.

"There are tracks everywhere... In the east, anyway," I said.

"It's called the Eastern Sub Transport Line. I'm guessing there's a Midwest and Western line, too," Wes said.

"Okay," Vance said. "So we've got more tunnels. Doesn't actually change things, does it?"

Wes stepped backed and looked up and down the platform. "It does if we can find one of the trains."

"How?" Vance asked.

"It'll save us a whole lot of walking."

"Assuming it runs, and that's a big assumption," Vance said.

"Everything else works down here," Wes said. "There's no reason to think the trains are any different." He snapped his fingers and pointed to a door. "Get the gorillas. We need to open that door."

I called for Ajax and Ariabod, and we all approached the door. There was no door knob or handle. No apparent way to open it.

"You two," Wes said to the gorillas, "do your thing."

Ajax and Araibod huffed and started pounding away on the door. After several minutes, they had made small dents in it, but it didn't come close to opening.

"Wait, wait, wait," Vance said. "That control panel upstairs. Maybe there's a button or something up there."

Wes shrugged and talked into the radio. "Gordy. Hello, Gordy."

A few seconds passed before the static cleared, and we heard. "Go for Gordy."

Wes snickered and said, "I need you to go into that little room up there and find the control panel that opened the door to the stairwell."

"Ten-four, on my way, over."

"Kid was made for talking on a two-way," Wes said with a wide grin.

"At the control panel, over," Gordy said.

"Ten-four," Wes said with a wink. "Do you see anything that says something about a door or control room or anything like that?"

A few seconds passed. "Negative, fat man. I don't see anything like that, over."

Wes grimaced. "What do you see then?"

"There's something about O-2 measurements, filtration system cycle monitor, traffic control, vending cage..."

Wes pushed the button and tried to cut him off. "Did you say traffic control?"

Gordy continued his list. "... septic system, maintenance, and emergency lighting, over."

Wes rolled his eyes. "Traffic control. Did you say traffic control?"

"Roger. It's a button, over."

"Push it."

"I will if you say over, over."

Wes growled. "Push the button or I'm going to crack your skull, over."

"That wasn't so hard was it? Pushing button now, over."

We heard a soft humming followed by the door lifting up and disappearing into the door jamb.

"Did it do anything, over?"

Wes smiled. "It sure did."

There was a brief moment of static before Gordy said, "You're welcome, over."

We stood in the open doorway. The lights flickered and blinked before staying on. The room was a little bigger than the control room upstairs, but not by much.

Wes nodded and said, "Here goes nothing" before he stepped inside. We all followed.

On the far wall was a large desk with dozens of small television monitors. The images on the screen had a green tint. The images on the screens would occasionally change.

"Security cams," Wes said. "Scattered throughout the tunnels. Must be a couple hundred of them."

Vance leaned down and watched one of the monitors. "Anyone see a train?"

I shifted my eyes from monitor to monitor. "I don't see one."

"What are those blinking lights?" Tyrone asked.

We all turned to him, and he pointed to a giant electronic map on the wall behind us. Red lights blinked at different points on the map.

Wes stepped toward it. "The trains."

Vance squinted. "Trains? I don't see any trains."

"Each blinking light represents a train," Wes said standing in front of the map. "The question is where are we on this map?"

I examined the map and pointed to an area that appeared to be a platform. "These numbers, they look like GPS coordinates."

Excitedly, Wes said, "They do. They do... Look for a platform with the same GPS numbers from the blueprint…"

"Here," I said pointing to an area on the map. "This is it."

Wes looked to where I was pointing and then followed the map to the closest blinking light. He smiled, "I guess we're going to Scranton after all."

"Guys," Tyrone said.

"How far is it to Scranton?" I asked, ignoring Tyrone.

"Thirty miles," Wes said. "Give or take."

"Thirty miles?" Vance said. "I can't huff it 30 miles on this leg."

Wes looked at the map closer. "We might not have to. There's an emergency track between the two sets of tracks."

"So?" Vance said.

"So," Wes said pointing to some words on the map. "It's called Emergency Track Way for Subterranean Remote Vehicle."

"Guys," Tyrone repeated.

Ignoring him again, Vance said, "Once again, I say so?"

"So," Wes said with a sigh. "Remote means it's controlled remotely, and I'm betting it can be controlled from this room…"

"Guys!" Tyrone shouted.

We all turned to him, a little shocked by the volume of his voice.

He pointed to the bank of monitors. "I just saw Lou."

Chapter Fourteen

We watched the monitor until it cycled through three times and never saw Lou. Tyrone insisted he knew what he saw. "It was her. I know it."

"Maybe," Vance said. "Or maybe it was just a shadow."

"It was Lou!" Tyrone said looking as though he would punch Vance at any second.

"Does Lou know about this place?" I asked.

"I didn't even know about this place," Vance said.

"I mean the warehouse. Did you ever bring her to the warehouse?"

He nodded. "Floyd, too. But we never found this subway."

"You never found it," Wes said. He scanned the monitors while he talked. "But, someone had those blueprints out on that table upstairs. I'm thinking Floyd found it and has been using it to move about. And, if he's using it, Lou probably is, too."

"Why wouldn't they use the trains?" I asked.

Wes shrugged. "Could be they don't know how to engage the third rail."

"The third rail?" Tyrone asked.

"It's what makes the train go. It's not to be toyed with. Fry you like an egg."

"It's hot?"

"High voltage hot," Wes said. "It ain't on right now."

"How do you know?" Vance asked.

"Because I spent some time up in New York in my younger days. You know when the third rail is engaged. It gives off a low humming sound. You ride the subway long enough you don't hear it, but when you first start riding, it's all you hear. Sounds like electrified death."

Tyrone and I walked outside the room and approached the edge of the platform.

"You hear anything?" I asked.

"Nope."

I yelled, "How do we turn it on?"

Wes stepped out of the room. "We have to find the main traffic control room."

"That ain't it?" Tyrone asked.

Wes joined us and looked up and down the tracks. "Nah, it's an auxiliary room. The main room's probably five times that size and with a good deal more panels and buttons and monitors and whatnot."

A flash of static filled the air and then Gordy's voice came over the two-way radio clipped to Wes's belt.

"Guys?"

Wes smiled and said, "You didn't say over."

"Um, there's something up here," Gordy's said sounding like he was very near crying.

"What something?" Wes asked.

"I don't... I'm not sure. I heard a noise."

"What kind of noise?"

"It was like a thud... I don't know... kind of sounded like something fell off a shelf."

Wes shook his head. "Something probably did fall off a shelf. They're jammed packed with crap. Air system kicked on or something and knocked something off a shelf. You worry too much."

"I'm not the only one worried. That little ninja kid is freaking out. And since he's deaf, I'm thinking it's not because he heard what I heard."

Vance poked his head out of the traffic control room. "If Minnow is freaking out, something's up. That kid is as cool as a cucumber until trouble shows up."

I started for the door leading upstairs.

"Hold up," Wes said. He clicked the button. "You and the kid make your way down here, Gordy."

"Okay."

Wes clipped the radio back to the belt. "This is as good time as any to get on our way. No sense in going and asking for trouble if we can avoid it."

Vance shook his head. "No way I'm leaving that warehouse behind. It's a freakin' gold mine."

Wes let out a small snort. "You think that's the only warehouse? This whole system was set up to survive something horrible topside. I'm guessing there are dozens, maybe even hundreds of warehouses scattered along this underground railway system."

"The problem is you're guessing," Vance said.

We heard a loud bang that diverted our attention to the stairwell.

Wes grabbed his two-way. "Gordy?"

Static.

"Gordy? What's going on?"

A series of clicks game over the radio.

"What's going on?" Tyrone asked.

Wes shook his head. "I don't know... I mean he's pushing the button to talk but…"

The radio clicked again only this time the channel stayed open. We heard some screaming and crashing sounds and then a strained voice said, "I have to pick up the kids at soccer practice today."

Wes cocked an eyebrow and said, "That doesn't make a lick of sense."

The color in Vance's face faded. "The Gore."

"What about them?" I asked.

"That's what I was talking about. They say stuff like that. The one's with human heads do anyway. They just spout off old memories."

I bolted for the door leading upstairs. I could hear the others on my heels, including the rapid clack-clack of Vance bringing up the rear.

Inside the stairwell, I hurdled the first three steps and was on my way to climb some more when I heard voices.

"The market is down sixteen points. How much more can it drop?"

"Don't put that in your mouth, sweetie."

"I used to date that guy in the glasses."

I signaled the others to be quiet and backed against the wall. Slowly, I eased up the next few steps, stretching my neck to get a good view at what was up the next flight of stairs. The voices stopped, but I could hear the fall of clumsy footsteps. When I reached the level that led to the next series of steps, the lights clicked off.

"Crap," Wes said from below in the dark.

"Glow sticks," Vance said.

I heard rustling as someone rummaged through a backpack.

"Got it," Tyrone said. The stick came alive with a bright green glow. "Here," he said tossing it up to me.

I reached for it but failed to catch it. It tumbled to the platform, and I quickly stooped down to pick it up. Only a few seconds passed, but it felt like an eternity. Once I found it, I stood and looked down the stairs. "Found it."

By that time, Vance and Wes were holding their own glow sticks. I did not like the expressions on their faces.

"Boy," Wes said. "Get down here now!"

"His name was Charlie," I heard a girl strain to say.

I stiffened and turned with the glow stick extended in front of me. There, just a few feet away, was a Gore. A teenage girl's head sat on top of a what appeared to be a horse's torso. It reached out for me with a man's meaty hands. I stumbled back and crashed down the stairs, hitting my head on the last step.

Tyrone jumped over me and started up the stairs.

"Back off, boy!" Wes said. "There's a pack of those damn things."

I blinked to get my focus back and saw what Wes was talking about. Two more Gore stepped up behind the one with the girl's head.

Tyrone hesitated and then backed off.

Wes helped me to my feet, and we all made our way back out onto the train platform.

"What do we do?" Tyrone asked. "We gotta get up the stairs to Gordy and the kid."

"Let those things funnel down here. They ain't the most agile things. Maybe we can get them down on the tracks."

"What'll that do?" Tyrone asked.

"It'll give us the high ground," Wes said. "We can have an easier time taking them out if they're below us."

I rubbed the pain out of the back of my head and then readied my crossbow. The first Gore crossed through the doorway. I raised it to fire, but Wes stopped me.

"No, no, let them through. We don't want them blocking the stairwell."

Three more of the Gore piled out of the door. They walked a few feet but stopped and then swayed back and forth. The dead eyes of the human heads stared at us.

A roar blasted through the tunnel system, but I couldn't tell where it came from. The hair on the back of my neck stood up. We all huddled together and backed towards the wall.

"Um, fellas," Vance said.

"What?" Wes said.

"I think we've been set up."

"What do you mean?" I asked.

He pointed toward the tunnel. "Granted my eyes suck, but I'd say that's a group of Gore headed our way."

I looked where he was pointing, and my chest nearly exploded from the racing of my heart.

"They trapped us," Vance said.

Ajax charged to the edge of the platform and pounded the pavement with his fists. Ariabod rose up and beat his chest.

Wes growled. "Are you saying they're that kind of smart? They set up a trap for us?"

"It appears so," Vance said. "And nothing against you guys, but we ain't got a chance without Minnow."

I fired an arrow at Gore coming up the tunnel. The arrow hit it square in the hand. The creature bellowed and screeched.

"Well, we've had a few scraps along the way," Wes said. "I like our chances." He fired an arrow and hit the same Gore in the other hand. It cried out even louder as one arm fell to the ground and then the other.

"The hands," I said. "Go for the hands."

Tyrone gripped his knife and slowly moved away from the group. "This is going to be fun." He took off in a full sprint toward the Gore standing near the stairwell. Just as he reached them, one of them swung its mangled arm and landed a blow across Tyrone's jaw. He tumbled to the side and fell to the ground, smacking his head on the concrete.

"You dang fool!" Wes screamed as he moved his fat frame forward.

Tyrone struggled to get on his hands and knees. He shook his head to clear the cobwebs and was about to stand when a Gore yanked him up by his forearm and held him dangling in midair.

"I have a meeting at 10:30. Can we meet after lunch?" The words came out of the human head's mouth. The flesh was decaying, but I could tell it was an older man.

Tyrone kicked and squirmed and tried to get loose.

Wes let out a battle cry as he stormed the Gore holding Tyrone.

To our rear, a half dozen Gore approached the platform from the tracks. When one got close enough to the platform, Ajax reached down and yanked its head from its body. The gorilla stared into the dead eyes of the horse and flung it as hard as he could at the back wall.

Another Gore placed its hand on the concrete floor and attempted to climb up on the platform, but Ariabod moved in quickly and twisted the creature's wrist until the hand tore free. The Gore fell back on the tracks.

"Let him loose," Wes shouted. He stalked the Gore that had a hold of Tyrone. The butt of his crossbow was propped up on his shoulder as Wes tried to get a bead on the monster's free hand.

One of the Gore approached him from the doorway. I quickly aimed my crossbow and fired, hitting it in the crook of the arm. The creature didn't even flinch. I loaded again and ran towards it.

Wes finally fired, and the arrow struck the Gore's thumb. The Gore shook its hand and the thumb dangled by a thin strip of dead skin.

I fired another arrow hitting the other Gore in the hand. It screeched and lurched back into the stairwell.

The Gore holding onto Tyrone followed.

I watched as Ajax and Ariabod prevented two more Gore from climbing up on the platform, but they couldn't prevent a third one from pulling itself up. The mangled creature lurched awkwardly toward Vance.

Vance saw it coming and readied his hunting knife. When he thought the Gore was close enough, he swung the knife wildly, but missed.

In the stairwell, Tyrone finally freed himself, but instead of running to safety, he grabbed the Gore's hand and twisted. His knife was on the floor near the door, but he wasn't about to let go of the Gore in order to retrieve it. He yanked the hand with all his might while the Gore desperately tried to jerk free.

The last Gore that had been blocking the doorway turned and rushed Tyrone. I fired an arrow and hit it in the wrist. Panicked, it ripped the arrow free and broke it in half.

Wes followed me into the stairwell. I ditched the crossbow and pulled my knife from my sheath. When the Gore grabbed for Tyrone to help the other Gore, I brought the blade down on its knuckles.

The Gore howled in pain and turned on me. Wes shot an arrow into its other hand and then pulled out his knife. Together, we rushed the creature and cut its hands free from its mismatched arms. Within seconds, the Gore's body parts fell away and formed a horrific pulsating pile.

Tyrone managed to rip the decaying flesh that connected the hand of the Gore to its spindly arm. The creature gave one last violent jerk and freed itself from Tyrone and its hand. It whimpered madly and scrambled to climb the stairs. By the time it reached the next level, Minnow appeared covered in blood and goo and sliced the Gore to pieces.

"Where's Gordy?" I asked him completely forgetting he couldn't hear me. I rushed up the stairs and grabbed him by the shoulders. "Gordy," I said slowly and loudly.

He pointed with his knife in the direction of the warehouse.

I turned to Wes and before I could say anything he shouted, "Go! We got this."

I moved past Minnow and navigated around the pieces of Gore scattered all over the stairs. By the time I reached the warehouse, my boots were covered in blood.

"Gordy!" I yelled. My voice echoed throughout the large room.

A scream came from the back.

I raced toward it with my knife drawn. The blood on my boots caused me to slip, and I almost fell a number of times before I reached the end of an aisle. I frantically untied the boots and kicked them off my feet. With my bare feet slapping the hard concrete floor, I continued down the aisle listening for another sign of Gordy.

"Oz!"

I stopped. "Gordy? Where are you?"

"Up here."

I looked up in the direction of his voice and saw him huddled in a quivering mass on the fifth shelf. "How did you get up there?"

"Dude, when you've got those Gore things chasing you, you'd be surprised how high and fast you can climb."

"Yeah, well, they're gone. You can come down."

He shook his head. "They're not gone."

Something fell from the shelf at the end of the aisle.

Gordy scooted farther back on the shelf. "You see?"

I nodded and whispered. "Yeah."

"Oz, dude, just climb up here," he whispered back.

I shook my head. "Can you see it?"

There was a moment of silence before he answered with a no. "Just climb up here already."

I quickly grabbed hold of the shelves and worked my way up to the second row. I stopped when I heard another loud bang.

"They're getting closer," Gordy said.

I climbed faster and reached the fourth row before we heard a crash. Several items fell from the shelves.

I peered down the aisle. "I don't understand why we can't see it."

Gordy didn't answer.

"It's gotta be right here. That stuff just came from a few shelves over." I pulled myself up to the fifth row and froze when I saw a small Gore holding Gordy by the throat. It was like the bigger Gore with the mismatched body parts only this one was designed to get around in small spaces. It had the head of a house cat. Looking past the Gore, it wasn't hard figuring out why we hadn't seen it. We had been searching the ground for it when it was moving towards us from the fifth row of shelves.

"Well, well, well," a voice said from below.

I looked down, and felt my blood boil at the sight of Floyd smiling back up at me from the warehouse floor. "Where's Lou?" I asked

"Lou?" His grin got bigger. "She's around somewhere. But I wouldn't concern yourself with her. She's got better things to do now. No time to think about silly matters such as boys and love and that kind of nonsense. She serves the Gore now."

I moved to climbed down the shelf, but stopped when Gordy squeaked in pain. The cat head Gore tightened its grip around Gordy's throat.

"Stay where you are, young man. We've got business."

"Tell this thing to let Gordy go."

Floyd laughed. "I could, but it wouldn't do any good."

"You're lying…"

"You've got things turned around, my friend. You think I tell the Gore what to do. I don't. I wouldn't dare. I'm just a meager, ugly human. The Gore are gods. I serve them, Oz. I serve them happily and completely. That's what servants do."

I inched toward Gordy and the Gore.

"I wouldn't do that," Floyd said.

He couldn't possibly see me from his vantage point.

"The cat heads are pretty fickle little guys. There's no telling what will set him off."

"What does it want?"

"Well, it wants your friend's head there, but luckily it's agreed to show some mercy."

"Then tell it to show it by letting Gordy go."

Floyd moved to the shelf behind him and grabbed a package of figs. "Most underappreciated snack ever," he said opening the package. "I could never figure out why figs weren't more popular. They're delicious. I used to make this fig pie…"

"Who cares?" I shouted.

He looked up at me with a mouthful of figs. "That was rude."

The Gore tightened its grip on Gordy's throat, making it even more difficult for Gordy to breathe.

"Okay, okay," I said. "I'm sorry."

The Gore loosened its grip.

Floyd smiled. "I get it. You're stressed out. This type of situation can do that to a person, but we mustn't forget our manners, Oz. No, sir, we must not forget our manners." He popped another fig into his mouth.

I wanted to jump off the shelf and beat the life out of him, but I took a deep breath and let it out in an attempt to calm myself. It didn't work. "What do you want us to do?"

He swallowed the fig before answering. "We want the boy."

"The boy?"

"Minnow. We want him."

I snickered. "He's just a little kid."

Floyd, irritated by my response, growled, "He's an abomination, a vile, corrupt little demon, and he must pay for the gods he's killed."

I noticed the dead eyes of the cat-head Gore. "These things have gotten into your head, Floyd. They're not gods…"

"Shut up!" he said frantically. "Shut up! Shut up! Shut up!"

When the echo from his rant quieted down, I heard the small Gore purring.

"You couldn't begin to understand how beautiful my gods are. You haven't the eyes to see such a thing. Only the blessed like me and your precious Lou can see it…"

"Listen to me, Floyd. We can help you. You can join us…"

"Join you?" He said bemused. "Why would I want to do a thing like that? I belong to the greatest power in this world. I was chosen to serve the Gore. Do you understand what that means? That means I am special. I am loved."

"They don't love you, Floyd…"

"Enough! The boy! We want the boy!"

The Gore moved backwards dragging Gordy with it.

"No, stop," I said.

"Your friend is ours."

The Gore's grip was too tight for Gordy to talk, but his eyes said everything. He was terrified.

"He stays. Gordy stays with me. I'll get you the boy. Just don't take Gordy."

The Gore continued to drag Gordy away.

"Do you have a watch?" Floyd asked as he grabbed another package of figs off the shelf.

I ignored his question and peered down at him. "Listen to me, Floyd. I've learned to do one thing very well since the world ended."

"A watch," he said, "Do you have one?"

Still ignoring him, I said, "I've learned how to be a killer, and I can promise you if you hurt Gordy I am going to give you an up close and personal demonstration."

He held up his watch and said very loudly and slowly, "Do you have a watch?"

"Why would I need a watch?" I shouted.

He tossed the watch up to me. "I'll give you 48 hours to bring us the boy. If you're one minute late, your friend joins the Gore." He started to walk away, but stopped. "Piece by piece."

I watched as he moved down the aisle biting into a fig. "Wait! How will I find you?"

He held up a walkie-talkie as he continued to walk. "I'll be in touch." He reached the end of the aisle. "Do yourself a favor and try the figs. They're spectacular."

Chapter Fifteen

The rest of the Gore disappeared into the tunnels not long after Floyd, and his small cat-head Gore vanished with Gordy in tow. I sat on the cold concrete floor of the underground warehouse. I wiped the sweat and blood from my hands and face with a towel Wes had pulled from the shelves.

Vance was in the control room cleaning all evidence of battle from Minnow's face. I watched them until a horrible feeling of guilt smashed my thoughts to bits. I was considering trading the boy for Gordy. I fought the idea, but every time I came to a dead end on how to get Gordy back, Floyd's voice made the demand in my head.

I hadn't told any of the others what Floyd had said. I didn't want them to know that he wanted the boy and that he was willing to give us Gordy back in exchange. I hadn't told them because I wasn't sure what I was going to do yet.

"He just dragged him off?" Wes asked, drinking some water from a plastic bottle.

I rested my head against the wall. "He didn't. A Gore did. A small one, had a cat head."

"And he said he'd get in touch with you on the radio when he was ready to talk?"

I nodded.

"Talk about what?" Tyrone asked. He was still amped up from the battle. I thought I almost detected a smile on his face.

"Getting Gordy back," I said. "He wants to make us an offer."

"What kind of offer?" Wes asked.

"I don't know," I said sharply. "He didn't say. He just said he'd be in touch."

"It doesn't make sense," Wes said. "What could he want?"

Tyrone jumped in quickly with an idea. "The warehouse. I bet that's what it is. He wants this warehouse."

Wes squeezed the water bottle and then slammed it against the wall. "He don't need our permission to take this damn place! He could just take it with those chunks of crud he's aligned himself with! It just doesn't make sense!"

Vance moved to the open doorway of the control room. "You're right."

We turned to him.

"The Gore aren't ones for negotiation. They should have plucked your friend apart and divided up his parts."

"They want the warehouse," Tyrone said.

"Not likely," Vance said. "Nothing in here does them any good."

I looked past him and watched as Ajax and Minnow signed to each other.

"They work for Floyd," Tyrone said. "He wants the warehouse…"

"They don't work for him," I said. "He works for them. He thinks they're gods."

"Gods?" Wes said with a sour expression. "Those things? They're as about as foul as you can get in both odor and appearance."

I shook my head. "Floyd doesn't see it that way. To hear him talk, there's nothing more beautiful."

Vance hobbled forward. "No use trying to figure it out. I spent some time with that crackpot. He's far gone. The Gore got into his head while he was still back in Charleston. He would've given up any piece of him they wanted, but for whatever reason they decided to use him as a… collector, I guess you'd call him. They use your friend Lou the same way."

Wes turned away from him. It killed him hearing that Lou was working for the Gore.

Tyrone didn't have a problem talking about it. "She's hacking up people for those things?"

Vance shrugged. "Well, with the exception of my hand, I can't say if she's made a general practice out of it. She mostly sticks to grave robbing and cutting up corpses. The Gore prefer fresh parts, but they'll make do with dead meat when they have to."

I stood and looked at the watch Floyd had given me. "We've got less than 48 hours to figure out how to get Gordy back. Let's not waste time talking about this crap."

"What do you suggest we do?" Vance asked.

"Find the Gore," I said. "Take the fight to them before they have a chance to bring it to us."

Vance chuckled.

"What's so funny?" I asked.

"Well," Vance said, "that's a pretty tall order. Find the Gore. I'm not sure if you've thought that through."

"What's the big deal? I saw you and Minnow up at your cabin. You all didn't seem to have much problem killing those things."

"That's because we lure them in one at a time. They're not so bad in broad daylight minus a part or two that Minnow manages to steal, but down here, in the tunnels with Floyd and your friend Lou working for them? Well, that's an entirely different story."

I recalled something he had said earlier about the Gore. "Why are they able to survive down here? I thought you said they wore themselves down and fall apart without resting during the day."

"They do need the rest. The sun helps them gauge how long they've rested, but they don't need the sun if they've got Floyd and Lou looking after them. Those two probably let the Gore know when it's time to power down and wake up."

Wes snapped his fingers. "That's the answer."

"What's the answer?" Tyrone asked.

"We don't need to find the Gore to save Gordy. We need to find Floyd and Lou."

Vance smiled. "That's an idea."

"If we get a hold of those two, tie them up or detain them in some way, it'll just be a matter of time before the Gore in the tunnels give out. How much time do we need?" Wes asked Vance.

"They can only go about 12 hours before they need to stack themselves in piles and rest."

I felt a little spark of hope. "That's the plan then." I turned to see Ajax and Minnow still engaged in conversation. The hope immediately gave way to shame. I knew that if we failed I'd still be willing to trade the kid for Gordy. It didn't feel like a Creyshaw thing to do.

Chapter Sixteen

We all gathered in the control room on the sub-level after loading up with weapons and supplies. Standing in front of the bank of monitors, we watched as the images cycled through.

"Do you remember anything about the image of Lou?" I asked Tyrone.

He kept his eyes glued on the monitors. "Maybe."

"Maybe?" Wes snapped. "You gotta do better than maybe."

"It was quick. I wasn't sure it was her at first. When I realized it was, the video changed."

Vance pointed at one of the monitors. "There… upper left hand corner… I can't see squat, but they should have camera numbers. Do you remember the number?"

Tyrone shook his head. "No. I'm not even sure which monitor I saw it on now. They all look the same."

"Did you see tracks? A train? A platform?" I asked.

"Asking me all these questions doesn't help," Tyrone said.

"We're just trying to jog your memory," Wes said.

Frustrated, Tyrone said, "I remember a big white spot, like a spotlight or something…" He stopped midsentence. "I remember something else, a can on the bottom of the screen, the right side, a big can."

"A big can? Like a coffee can?" Vance asked.

Excitedly, Tyrone said, "Yes, a coffee can, that's what it was. I remember it now. Lou stepped over it."

We all focused on the monitors in front of us. There was no order. No one was assigned a specific bank of monitors. We were just determined to spot a coffee can on the ground on one of the screens.

"C'mon," Tyrone said. "I know I saw it…"

"There!" I shouted pointing at the last monitor on the far left. "Camera 62! I saw it!"

"Sixty-two," Wes said flipping through a notebook that was attached to the side of the table with a thin plastic covered cable. "Are you sure?"

"Positive."

Wes flipped through the notebook and found the section that linked the location of the cameras with their numbers. He mouthed the number over and over as his finger ran down the page. "Sixty-two," he finally said out loud. "Section 1233, westbound bravo."

"Where the hell is that?' Tyrone asked.

Wes moved to the blinking map on the wall. His eyes darted from section to section until he spotted it. Pointing, he said, "There it is." He counted in his head. "It looks like there's six platforms between us and it."

"What's that in miles?" I asked.

He shrugged. "Fifteen, maybe twenty."

"What are the chances we can find that emergency remote vehicle?" Vance asked.

Wes smiled. "Pretty good considering we found a coffee can the size of a dot on a monitor that's about the size of a slice of bread." He moved to the control panel. "Find the word 'remote.'"

Minutes passed as we all studied the control panel. Vance bent down and practically put his face on the panel in order to read the various labels on the buttons. He stopped over one particular button and studied it. He then moved away from it, only to come back to it.

"What do you suppose REV means?" He asked.

There was a moment of silence before Tyrone answered. "Like rev your engines. Maybe it makes the trains go faster."

"Then why are the letters all caps?" Vance looked up from the panel.

"REV," Wes said to himself. "Remote Emergency Vehicle! Push it. Push the button."

Vance smiled and did as Wes suggested.

Nothing happened.

We ran to the platform and listened for any signs that the emergency vehicle was approaching.

"How big is it?" Tyrone asked.

Wes shrugged. "Can't say for sure. Most of the ones I've seen have been converted pickup trucks, more or less. Instead of tires, they've got wheels like you'd find on a train."

I heard a grunt from the control room and looked inside. Ajax, Ariabod, and Minnow were staring at the monitors. I joined them and immediately saw what had them so captivated. As the images on the monitors cycled through, you could see the emergency vehicle moving down the middle track.

I yelled for Wes.

He came back into the control room followed by Vance.

"It's coming," I said pointing at the monitors.

He smiled. "You doubted me? Son, if it's got wheels and a motor, I know how to make it go." He moved closer to the monitors and studied the car as it moved from image to image. "Huh?"

"What?" Vance asked.

"Well, the good news is it is indeed headed this way, and there's room enough for all of us. The bad news is there appears to be someone already in it."

Chapter Seventeen

The thought and hope that the person in the emergency vehicle might be Lou crossed all our minds. The reality was that the way things generally went for us in this world the best bet was that it was something or someone we didn't know, and it most likely wanted to kill us.

I jumped down on the tracks, crossed the middle set of tracks and found an archway where I could hide. My crossbow was loaded and ready to fire.

Tyrone climbed down the platform and found a place to hide on that side of the tunnel. Vance held Minnow back at the control room while Wes and the gorillas stood in plain sight. Wes had his crossbow at the ready, too. Our hope was that whatever was in the emergency vehicle would be so focused on what was on the platform it wouldn't even think to look for anyone on the tracks.

A repetitive clanging sound echoed throughout the tunnel signaling the arrival of the modified truck. I counted the clangs. By the time I got to four, I could see the headlights of vehicle round a bend. Taking a step out of the shadows, I waved to the others to let them know that it was coming.

Wes propped his crossbow on his shoulder and placed his finger on the trigger. I stepped back into the shadows and did the same. Tyrone crouched down behind a thick concrete pillar and held his knife at the ready.

The yellow truck continued clanging over the tracks, slowing as it got closer to our platform. I pressed my back against the cool, damp wall when the emergency vehicle came to a stop in front of me.

We waited for the occupant to come out. But whoever or whatever it was just sat there. I slowly leaned forward to get a better view, but I couldn't make out anything.

I heard the sound of rocks being displaced and watched as Tyrone stepped out from behind the pillar. He craned his neck to get a look in the truck. His brow furrowed, and he took another step. He stood straight and said, "Hey."

The occupant of the truck didn't move.

"Hey, you," Tyrone said moving in closer.

"Careful," Wes said.

Tyrone opened the passenger side door of the emergency vehicle. I watched as he leaned inside and then said, "Whoa!"

"What is it?"

"Dead guy," Tyrone said as he quickly stepped back and put his hand over his face. "A very smelly dead guy."

I stepped forward. "You sure he's dead?"

"He's dead. Trust me."

Wes eased up and pointed the crossbow toward the ground. "Now, I wish I could say that settles it, but there are degrees of dead in this place. Is he kind of dead or completely dead?"

Tyrone examined the corpse. "He's about as dead as you can get, even for this place."

We all converged on the truck. The man had been dead for a while. His skin was gray and clammy. His eyes were shut underneath a pair of black-rimmed glasses with thick lenses, but his mouth was wide open, revealing a swollen tongue that had turned purple. He was wearing a uniform of some kind.

"Must've worked down here," Wes said. He reached in and pulled the glasses off the dead man's face. He cleaned them off with his shirttail before handing them to Vance. "These might help you see."

Vance put the glasses on and blinked several times in an attempt to bring his surroundings into focus. "Well, it's better. Things have gone from blurry to fuzzy."

Wes patted him on the back. "You're better off not getting us too much in focus. We lost all our pretty when Lou left."

Tyrone reached in and tugged on the dead man's collar to try and pull him out of the truck. "He's heavy for a skinny dead guy."

Wes helped him. After several seconds and a great deal of effort, they dragged the man out of the truck and laid him on the ground.

"What do we do with him?" Vance asked. "Seems like we should bury him or something."

"Why?" Tyrone asked.

Vance was puzzled by his question. "What do you mean why? It's the decent thing to do, that's why."

Tyrone shrugged off Vance's judgmental tone. "We're on a pretty tight schedule. Seems kind of stupid to take the time to bury some guy we didn't know."

Wes sighed. "While I don't necessarily agree with the way young Tyrone is saying it, I do agree with him. We don't really have the time to give this fella a proper send off. We can lay him off under that archway over there and say a word or two about him, and then we best be on our way."

Vance grumbled to himself and then threw up his hands. "I can't bury him by myself so I'll go along with your suggestion."

"No," I said.

Everyone turned to me.

"We could use him."

I got a mixture of disgusted and confused stares.

"Lou's collecting for these Gore things, right?"

Vance nodded.

"I say we use our new friend there as bait to draw her out."

"Bait?" Vance said horrified.

Tyrone nodded with a grin. "That could work."

"That could work?" Vance looked to Wes to join him in his disgust.

Wes thought about my plan and then scanned all our faces before saying, "It's not a bad idea."

"What is wrong with you people?" Vance shouted. "This is a person we're talking about."

"A dead person," Tyrone said.

"It's still a person…"

"You burn body parts like they're firewood," Tyrone said with a touch of anger.

"Gore infected body parts," Vance said. "They're not exactly dead or human."

"I know it sounds a might cold," Wes said, "but we've gotta think of the end game here. We get Lou we get closer to Floyd. We get closer to Floyd we've got a chance to save Gordy. I say that's worth using this poor dead fella as bait."

Vance crossed his arms and said, "I hate to say it, but Gordy is part of the Gore now."

"What do you mean by that?" Wes asked.

"I mean he's been divided up into pieces and has taken his place in the piles by now. They've severed every part of him and put him to good use. This mission you're going on is nothing more than a trap. Floyd is leading you deeper into the tunnels and then he's going to ambush you."

I felt like strangling him, but I held myself back. "You don't really believe that."

"What makes you think that?"

"Because you would have said something by now. You wouldn't have been planning to come with us, and you especially wouldn't agree to get Minnow involved in this if you thought it was a trap."

He nearly growled in frustration. "Let's just say I've come to my senses. This is a stupid plan. Gordy's dead. End of story." He backed away. "Now, I'm taking Minnow, and we're going back up to the warehouse."

"No, you're not," I said calmly but coldly.

"The kid's my responsibility. I was an idiot for going along with you as far as I have…"

"They want Minnow," I said cutting him off.

Stunned, Vance stared at me without saying a word.

"What do you mean they want Minnow?" Wes asked.

"They want to make a trade, Gordy for Minnow." I said it so low that I wasn't sure anyone heard me. I was too ashamed to even look at them.

"That's not true," Wes said with an expression of disbelief on his face. "You would have told us something like that. Wouldn't you, Oz?"

I hesitated trying to find the right words to make me seem like less of an ass, but there was nothing I could say to make me come off better. "I wanted to sort it all out myself before I said anything."

"You were just biding your time," Vance said. "You were sucking me and Minnow in on your rescue mission so you could hand over the boy for your precious Gordy."

"That's not it..."

"Bull crap that ain't it!" Vance said. Spit was coming out of his mouth he was so angry. His voice seemed to nearly collapse the tunnel walls. "I've seen liars, kid. I was a liar. I know when someone's working his own deal. You almost had me fooled with this hero nonsense, but you're a monster just like any other in this world. This is all about you and your people. Vance and Minnow don't amount to specs of dust in your eyes."

"Hold on!" Wes said, his face and eyes red. "Oz, ain't like that at all. He didn't tell us, sure, but I know the boy. He had his reasons."

"Fine," Vance said. "Let's hear them then."

I looked at both men and tried not to get angry. I had no right to get angry, but they were backing me into a corner. "My reasons for not telling you what the Gore wanted... I... I'm not..."

Vance waved me off and started to hobble toward the platform. "Me and Minnow are out of here."

"I don't know what I'm doing!" I shouted so loud I scared myself. I collected my thoughts while the echo of my voice bounced around the tunnel. "I want to do the right thing. I do. I swear I do. I just don't know what that is. Gordy is my friend, my best friend. He's a jerk and annoying, and he contributes almost nothing to the group, but he would be dead without us. I'm supposed to protect those kinds of people, right? I mean that's why we're here in the first place. I didn't protect the people I should have. Worse than that. I bullied those people, people like Stevie. I am a monster. I know that. But I'm trying not to be. I just thought I'd figure something out before we ran out of time. I thought some kind of brilliant plan would come to me, and if we get to Floyd and Lou… It could work, but it might not…"

"And if it doesn't?" Vance asked. "What then?"

"Then I'll do what it takes to save Gordy."

Vance shook his head in disgust. "Some hero. You'd sacrifice a small boy…"

"Not just him," I said. "You, me, Wes, all of us. I'm tired of losing people, and I won't lose anymore. We get Gordy back, or we all die trying. That might not be the right thing to do, but if it's what has to be done, it's what we'll do."

"Well, me and Minnow are out of the 'we' business. Goodbye and good luck to you."

I had the crossbow trained on him before he could move. "You can go, but Minnow stays."

Vance's face turned beet red. He gripped his pitchfork.

"What the hell are you doing, boy?" Wes yelled.

"What I have to."

"This ain't the way," he said. "Move that damn thing off Vance."

"We have to stop pretending this gets done without getting ugly," I said.

"Pretending… What in the hell are you talking about, Oz? This thing's been ugly since day one. You remember day one, don't you? When we was fighting them butt-faced Greasywhoppers? We, Oz. You and me and every one of us. We did that. We beat them back, too. Because we worked together without pointing weapons at one another. You gotta stop this thing from falling apart in your head. Stay with me, boy. Stay with me."

I thought about what he said and slowly lowered my weapon.

Vance breathed a little easier. "What the hell is a Greasywhopper?"

Wes and I were too exhausted from the tension to answer so Tyrone jumped in. "They were these big greasy, hairy things with big mouths and bigger teeth. Only they aren't really called Greasywhoppers. That was the name Wes came up with. We couldn't call them by their real name."

"Why not?"

Tyrone shrugged. "I can't remember."

"Because," I said. "They couldn't find you if you didn't say their name."

Tyrone snapped his fingers. "That's right. I remember now. They just came out of nowhere. But we fixed that. Once Oz took out their queen, we could say their name without worrying."

Wes chimed in. "This is a nice little trip down memory lane, but we still got to settle this business with the Gore."

I was about to apologize to Vance when I caught sight of Ajax and Minnow signing to each other. Ajax was going a million miles a minute and Minnow appeared as if he was trying to calm the gorilla down. Suddenly, the boy ran into the control room.

I started walking towards them. "What's going on?"

Ajax grunted and signed to me as frantically as he had been signing to Minnow.

"I've got no idea what you're saying, big guy."

"Something's got him riled," Wes said.

Minnow hurried out of the control room holding a piece of paper. Reaching the edge of the platform, he stomped his foot and held out the piece of paper.

"What do you think he wants?" Tyrone asked.

"Whatever it is, it's urgent," Wes said.

Tyrone shrugged and plodded toward the platform. He gave Minnow the once-over before he reached up and took the paper from him. He looked at it and let out a "Huh."

"What is it?" I asked.

"A note. I didn't know he could write. Did you?"

"He doesn't do it much. Only if he has to," Vance said.

"What does it say?" I asked.

Tyrone read it to himself again and then said, "Ajax says 'don't say their name.'"

A chill went down my spine.

"Don't say whose name?" Vance asked.

Wes looked at me. He was as unsettled by the phrase as I was.

"Doesn't say," Tyrone said. "We used to not be able to say the Takers' name, but those guys are big pussy cats now..."

Ajax let out a warbled roar. He started to pace on the edge of the platform. I could tell he wanted to pound Tyrone within an inch of his life.

"What's got into you?" Tyrone asked Ajax.

I ran over to Tyrone and ripped the note out of his hands. "That was the name you weren't supposed to say."

"What? Why? They aren't scary anymore. They work for the Délons. Right? I mean isn't that how it works..."

I heard a sound coming from the tunnel behind him. "Shhhh."

It took a few seconds for the echo of our voices to die down. A few seconds more, and I heard the sound again. A clicking sound. A few seconds more and we heard a chorus of clicking.

Vance stepped toward the sound. "What in the hell is that?"

Ajax, Ariabod, and Minnow climbed off the platform.

"They're here," I said.

"Appears that way," Wes said, sounding nervous and unsure.

"A lot of them," Tyrone said.

"Someone want to clue me in?" Vance said.

"Ta..." Wes started to say their name, but stopped himself even though it clearly didn't matter now. "The Greasywhoppers are here."

Vance held out his pitchfork. "What do we do?"

"We find some distance between us and them," Wes said moving to the emergency vehicle. He reached inside and examined the controls. "There's a manual override. Let's get in this thing and go."

Vance groaned. "This ain't fair. You people fixed this so me and Minnow would have to go."

We all converged on the truck.

"No one fixed anything," I said. "You want to stay? Stay. Minnow's coming with us."

"The hell he is. We'll take our chances up top..."

He screeched and fell to the ground.

An enormous hairy, clawed hand was sticking out of the ground and was wrapped around his ankle.

Minnow shot forward like with his knife drawn, ready to hack away.

Ajax lurched in front of him and knocked him to the ground while Ariabod barreled across the tracks and grabbed the wrist of the Taker that had a hold of Vance.

Vance screamed and yelped as he tried to pull free.

"Get in the truck!" Wes yelled.

Tyrone was in the bed of the truck before Wes had time to yell again, which he did. "We've gotta move! Now! Now! Now!"

Ariabod snapped the Taker's wrist, and the monster let go of Vance. Ariabod quickly snatched him up by his collar and pulled him to the truck. Ajax shoved Minnow into the cab.

A dozen or so glowing green eyes appeared at the bend in the tracks. Once I helped Vance on the bed of the truck, I slapped the roof and yelled, "Go, go, go!"

There was a small popping sound before the emergency vehicle slowly moved along the tracks. It seemed to be going as slow as a turtle. I tensed up as I watched the eyes get bigger and bigger in the darkness.

"Go!" Tyrone said. "Faster!"

"It can't take off like that," Wes said. "It's gotta ease into a good speed."

"Ease?" Tyrone said. "We don't have that kind of time."

A single Taker stepped into the light. It was bigger than I remembered, wider, thicker. They looked like Takers on steroids.

"Holy…" Vance started.

"They've changed," Tyrone said.

"And not for the better," I said slapping the roof. "Anything you can do to make this thing move faster, Wes, I suggest you do it now!"

I felt the wind pick up. We were going faster. The intermittent sounds of the wheels scooting across the sections of track got closer and closer together. The Takers were getting farther away.

Tyrone laughed like a lunatic. "Yes! We're home free!"

"Don't get too excited," I said. "We may have gotten away this time, but we've still got a major problem."

"What's that?" Vance asked.

"The Takers are back."

Chapter Eighteen

We must have traveled ten miles before we completely lost the sense that the Takers were still chasing us. They slinked back into their universe and were waiting for us to say their name again. They would have to wait a long, long while.

Wes pulled the emergency vehicle to a stop in front of a loading platform, and we all took the opportunity to catch our breaths and collect our thoughts. Vance shot me an evil eye whenever he caught a glimpse of me. I thought about trying to smooth things over with him, but I didn't know how.

"What now?" Tyrone finally asked.

"Nothing's changed," Wes said. "We get to Lou someway."

"We lost our bait," Tyrone said.

"That we did," Wes said.

I looked towards the platform and noticed a doorway with a sign that said 'Surface.' "There might be more," I said.

The others turned to the door.

"What'cha thinking?" Wes asked.

"The Gore," I said, "they're all over, right?" I directed my question to Vance, but he ignored me.

"Answer the boy," Wes said.

"I will not," Vance said. "I will not speak to him."

Wes growled and shook his head. "We ain't got time for this. Tell me if you won't talk to him. Are those Gore things all over?"

Vance shrugged. "They've been everywhere I've been."

I headed for the platform. "Then we head to the surface, find one, and bring pieces of it down here. That might draw Lou out."

"It'll do more than that," Vance said. He accidently looked at me and then quickly turned to Wes. "That'll most likely bring a gaggle of Gore down on us."

"What are you talking about?" I asked. "That's all you and Minnow did. You stole body parts off those piles."

Vance didn't respond.

"The boy said..." Wes started, but Vance cut him off.

"You tell him that the name Minnow isn't ever to come out of his mouth again!"

Wes sighed. "He said..."

"I heard him, Wes. I'm standing right here."

"Oh." He chortled despite the fact he was on edge. "I guess you are."

"As for what me and Minnow do," Vance said. "Like I said before, we do it up top in the open on our territory. They like to stay hidden, so at the most we've had to deal with one or two at a time. You're talking about bringing pieces of Gore down in these tunnels where we'll be sitting ducks."

"We don't really have time to worry about the risks." I moved to the platform and pulled myself up.

"You don't have time to worry about the risks?" Vance asked, forgetting that he wasn't speaking to me. "You better damn well worry about the risks. Because if you don't, we're all going to be part of the Gore."

The two gorillas moved to the platform. Ajax climbed on top of Ariabod and then hoisted Minnow up on his back. The little ninja was standing on the platform just as I stood and wiped the dirt and grime from my hands. He pulled his knife out from underneath his coat.

"I'm guessing the little guy smells Gore," Tyrone said.

"Stop that!" Vance shouted. "Minnow! Come back here!"

"Dude," Tyrone said, making his way to the platform. "You know he can't hear you, right?"

Vance stomped his rifle butt leg down on the ground. "Damn it!" He hobbled to the platform. "Send him back down here," he said to Tyrone.

Tyrone shrugged. "Kid can do what he wants."

He turned to me. "Send Minnow back down here. Don't take him with you."

The two gorillas climbed up on the platform. Ajax immediately started to sign with Minnow.

"He's not only going, but he's taking charge," I said.

Ajax huffed and nodded his head with a big grin across his face. He, Ariabod, and Minnow moved toward the door.

"Kid doesn't waste time," Tyrone said.

I instructed Wes to guard the truck.

Vance made his way to the platform. "I'm coming with you."

"No," I said. "Stay here with Wes."

"I'm not leaving Minnow in your care…"

I squatted down. "You have my word I won't let anything happen to him."

"I'm supposed to believe you? You were going to hand him over to the Gore…"

"That was then. I'm telling you now. Nothing will happen to him."

Wes lowered the truck's tailgate and sat down. "If Oz says he'll look after the boy, he'll look after the boy. Doesn't matter what happened before. His word is gold."

I stood, gave Vance the best reassuring nod I could, and joined the others in the stairwell leading up to the surface. Minnow was leading the way. I grew nervous whenever he would disappear around the corner to climb the next level of stairs. I couldn't let anything happen to him. And not just because I told Vance I wouldn't. I had to prove to myself that he meant something to me, that he was more than just a bargaining chip. I didn't want to believe that I would trade his life for Gordy's. I wasn't that kind of monster.

"Where do you think this comes out?" Tyrone asked as we got closer and closer to the surface.

"Don't know," I said. "I wouldn't be surprised if we end up on the Moon."

Tyrone stopped. "That couldn't happen, could it?"

"No," I said. "Probably not."

He rolled his eyes and continued to climb the stairs.

We reached a door that opened up into a room barely big enough for all of us. I pushed my way to the front and reached the door handle just as Minnow was about to reach for it. He was startled and relieved that I was going through the door first. He wasn't as fearless as he pretended.

The door opened into a short narrow hallway that lead to another door. With the others following close behind, I moved quickly to the next door, took a deep breath, and pushed it open. The space was dark. I felt something tug on my pant legs, and I turned to see Minnow holding a glow stick up to me. I took it, bent it to activate it, and held it out in front of me.

"Well?" Tyrone asked. "Where are we?"

I scanned the area and saw pipes and boxes everywhere. There was a damp, musky smell in the air. "It looks like a basement."

Slowly I walked deeper into the room. Tyrone and Minnow were holding up glow sticks to help push back the darkness. Together we generated enough light to reveal that we were indeed in a basement. I moved farther from the door and eventually found a staircase.

"Holy crap," Tyrone said. "How many stairs are we going to have to climb?"

"As many as it takes," I said starting my climb.

When I reached the top, I placed my hand on the door handle and groaned. I was getting fatigued from the stress of climbing out of the darkness and waiting to discover what waitedfor us on the other side of closed doors.

"What's the hold up?" Tyrone asked, sounding like he was out of breath.

I hesitated and then said, "I am."

"Let me through. I'll open the door."

"No," I said sharply. "I just need to rest for a second."

"Day's getting shorter, boss, and Gordy's time is ticking on by."

I scowled and threw my shoulder into the door. It opened up into a wide hallway. The floors were dusty, but underneath there was a polished concrete. The walls were made of oak, and wooden benches sat next to doors on either side of the hall.

We all stood in the large open hallway examining every inch of if before we dared take a step.

"Fancy," Tyrone said.

"It's some kind of government building, courthouse maybe."

Tyrone nodded. "Makes sense. Maybe that secret underground railroad was built to transport dangerous prisoners or famous judges or something."

I shrugged and followed the gorillas as they slowly knuckle-walked down the hallway. The building had not had visitors in a long time, and it almost seemed startled by our presence. A couple of times I got the feeling something was watching us. If I turned my head quickly, I thought I saw shadows zip out of sight.

At the end of the hallway, there was a door that opened up into a large circular atrium lined with huge windows that were caked with mud and dirty snow. I spotted a plaque to my left and read it out loud, "Northampton County Courthouse."

"Where's that?" Tyrone asked.

Next to the plaque was the state seal of Pennsylvania. "Somewhere in Pennsylvania," I said pointing at the seal.

Tyrone approached the large glass doors and did his best to wipe away a spot where he could see out. "Can't even tell if it's day or night."

He pushed and pushed until the door opened about two inches. "Cold," he said. "Colder than New Jersey."

"What do you see?" I asked.

"Snow. It's piled high, too. That's what's making opening this door so hard."

"Is it day?" I asked as I approached him.

He nodded. "Barely. I'd say it'll be dark in another thirty or forty minutes. And when I say dark, I mean dark. I can't even see the sky because of the clouds."

"We better get going then," I said. I directed Ajax and Ariabod to push the door open. Instead, they ripped it from the frame.

"That'll work," Tyrone said stepping through the open doorway.

I stood behind him and scanned the snow covered terrain.

"I hate to say it, Oz, but this is just about impossible. We'll never find the sidewalk much less a hidden pile of body parts."

Minnow squeezed past us and started making his way through the thick snow. He reached the end of a slope and stood. His head was snapping back and forth. After a few seconds, he pointed to his left with his knife and looked at us.

"We might not find one, but he will," I said.

Minnow headed left before all of us even got through the door.

"Hey!" I yelled. "Wait!"

"He can't hear you, boss," Tyrone said.

"Right." Turning to Ajax I said, "Go stop him and tell him to wait for us."

Ajax huffed and barreled through the loose snow towards Minnow. Fresh powder flew through the air as if being displaced by a plow. By the time he caught up with Minnow, they were at what appeared to be a street corner. The snow was so deep it was impossible to tell. There did appear to be the top edge of a stop sign sticking out of the top, soft layer of snow.

Minnow looked left and then right. If it we'd been in normal times, and the roads were cleared, he could have been a kid looking both ways before he crossed the street.

We were just a few feet away when he took off again with Ajax close behind. They headed for a row of what we thought were bushes. The closer we got the more we realized they weren't bushes. They were the tops of trees.

Minnow picked up his pace. Even Ajax struggled to keep up with him. His extra weight put him at a disadvantage as he sank deeper in the snow. I was afraid that if we ran into trouble he'd be too exhausted to defend himself.

I lost sight of Minnow when he rounded the tops of the trees. "Hey!"

Ajax made his turn around the tree tops, and he was gone, too, but only after letting out a hoot-grunt that told me he was in trouble.

When we made our way around the tree tops, we came upon a hole in the snow. It was large enough for a small boy and even a large gorilla to fall through.

"Ajax!" I yelled. It was impossible to see anything beyond the opening of the hole. It was pitch black.

There was no reply.

I called for him again.

This time I heard a grunt.

A few seconds passed, and Minnow activated a glow stick.

I strained to assess the situation.

"It's an office or something," Tyrone said.

I laid on the snow and stuck my head through the hole. Tyrone was right. It was an office of some kind. There was a metal desk, a computer and a cushioned chair. I pushed myself up on my knees and looked around. "I think it's a convenience store or something. They must have fallen through the roof down into the manager's office."

"How do we get them out?" Tyrone asked.

I shrugged and looked back in the hole. Ajax and Minnow were gone. "Where'd they go?"

Tyrone scooted on his belly and peered down in the hole. "Ajax!"

When there was no reply from the gorilla, Ariabod shoved me aside and jumped into the hole.

Tyrone repositioned himself and dangled his feet into the hole. "Nothing left to do but go down the hole." With that, he dropped himself down.

I hurriedly followed. Once my feet were on solid ground, I readied my crossbow and handed Tyrone a glow stick. He activated it and scanned the room. "Call me crazy, but it's almost hot in here."

I took a moment to gauge the temperature. "You're not crazy."

He opened his coat to cool off and then headed for the open doorway.

I was to follow when I saw him stop dead in his tracks. "What?"

He didn't answer. I could see his cheeks turn bright red.

"What is it?"

Instead of replying, he slowly ventured forward.

"Tyrone."

I heard Ariabod roar, and I quickly moved through the open doorway. It led to the back of the convenience store. Standing next to a row of empty shelves was a single Délon holding Minnow by his throat. The little ninja's knife was at the Délon's feet, and the boy struggled to free himself. Ajax and Ariabod paced on either side of the Délon growling and hooting. Tyrone slowly moved in closer. The source of the heat was now evident, a series of large metal trash cans were placed throughout the room, all of them filled with burning trash. The Délon had placed holes in the ceiling throughout the store to give the smoke a way to escape. Water from melting snow dripped down in a steady flow from the holes.

"Put him down," I said, my crossbow trained on him.

"That wouldn't be prudent," the Délon said. "He is providing me with protection. As long as I have the boy, you will not attack."

I stepped to my left and tried to find a clean shot. The Délon stepped with me, lifting Minnow off the ground and hugging him to his chest.

"This ends badly for you either way," I said.

"Why must you be so antagonistic, Oz?"

I dropped the crossbow just a hair. "Do we know each other?"

"We do," he said. "Or we did when I was as loathsome and pathetic as you in my human skin."

I tried to see through its grotesque purple complexion.

"You have grown," he said. "Can't call you a boy any longer. You are Oz the man. How unfortunate you have not let your Délon blood flow freely."

"He's messing with you, Oz," Tyrone said.

The Délon turned to Tyrone and studied him. "You are unknown to me. You are not from that wretched place I am from. Well, where my old human self is from."

"What wretched place is that?" I asked.

The Délon laughed. "Tullahoma of course."

My heart felt like it skidded to a stop. "You're from Tullahoma?"

A horrible smile spread across his face, "Shall I show you a face you will remember?" He closed his dead eyes and strained until the purple in his checks went away. The spider leg hairdo morphed into human hair. I watched in horror as the face of the Délon became my father's.

"Dad?"

"Son," he said still retaining the build and frame of a Délon.

I raised the crossbow but only to conceal the fact that I was crying.

"You have been so bothersome to General Roy. He sent me to strike a deal. He thought I would be able to get through to you."

"He thought wrong," I said.

"At least hear me out."

"No."

"There is a war, Oz."

"I know."

"Order has been undone. Destroyers are vying for control."

"None of this sounds like my problem," I said.

"How'd you get this far north?" Tyrone asked. "Isn't it too cold for you?"

"Terribly so," my father the Délon answered. "Despicably cold. But you forget we are in possession of a great many of those who created this world. We can make certain arrangements that suit us thanks to them and our ability to… convince them. They do have their limits however. Their 'fixes' tend to be inadequate and temporary. I nearly expired before I made it here."

"Why this store? You act like you knew we'd be here," I said.

"I did," he said. His face began to shudder, and his features changed back to Délon.

"How?" I asked.

"How does one know anything in this world?" He reached behind him still holding onto a squirming Minnow with one arm. When he brought his free arm forward, he was holding a homemade comic book. "It's called The Gore."

Tyrone and I shared a look.

"Vile creatures, the Gore," the Délon said.

"All the Destroyers are."

He chuckled. "I suppose that's true, but as far as we know, the Gore are not Destroyers. Not a race that belongs here at any rate."

"So," Tyrone said. "Stevie and his pals got bored and made other comic books with different kinds of monsters."

"Oh they did that, yes," the Délon said. "Several times over in fact, but none of them belong in this world. They shouldn't be here."

"So how'd they get here?" I asked.

"I told you order has been undone. You interfered where you shouldn't have, son…"

"Don't call me that," I said with a growl.

"There was a way this was to work. One Storyteller, one Destroyer, and One Creyshaw. Those were the rules from the beginning."

"I was supposed to just stand by and let you have your way."

"Yes!" the Délon shouted. "Yes! Yes! Yes! That is the way this was set up from the beginning. You were to beat the Takers, and we were to rule for all time!"

"I beat the Takers because it was written that way."

"And, it was written that way because Délons were meant to rule this world."

"This world shouldn't exist!"

He crowed. "Shouldn't it? Isn't this the world that existed all along?"

I watched as Ajax inched his way farther behind the Délon.

"The world you're so fond of, the one you want to return to, wasn't it crueler than this one? You've said as much, haven't you?"

I slowly took a single step forward. "I may have, but I was wrong. There are good people in my world."

"But you weren't good, were you?" The Délon noticed us trying to close in on him, so he squeezed Minnow tighter. The little Ninja squealed in pain.

I stopped and dropped the crossbow to my waist. "No, I wasn't."

"Yet you're good here. Are you not?"

"Am I? I don't feel good."

"You're good, Oz," Tyrone said. "Don't let him get in your head."

I nodded to Tyrone to let him know that I was all right.

"Your fellow human is right. You are good. Here, in this world, you are a champion. You fight for those who can't fight for themselves. You fight for your friends, your warriors. You are good."

"What's your point?" I asked annoyed.

"I'm just confused. Why would you want to return to a place where you aren't a Creyshaw? Where you are known for your cruelty? You are the boy who badgered poor Stevie Dayton into killing himself…"

"You don't think I've learned anything in this stinking place. I wouldn't be the same person. I'd be better. I'd be nicer to people like Stevie."

"Are you sure about that?" He pointed to the counter near front the door. "I've read differently."

I turned to where he was pointing. "What are you talking about?"

"Another one of Stevie's comic books. It features you again. You were one of his favorite topics after all."

I spotted the comic book next to the 'Lotto' sign.

"In this one, you leave this place. You go home, back to where you long to be. I am in my ugly human form. Your mother, too. We're all there. Living like lowly, pathetic human beings. Happy." He shivered. "Makes me ill just thinking about it."

I moved toward the counter. "We make it back?"

"You do."

"All of us?"

The Délon smirked. "Now, now. I won't give up any spoilers. I'll say only this. You are no different."

I stopped. "What?"

"Apparently Stevie thinks you are beyond redemption. You are just as cruel as you ever were. He is no longer there to bully, but you have a new poor soul to torture."

I waited for him to tell me who this poor soul was.

He paused just long enough to make me sweat. "The very Storyteller you fought so valiantly to save suffers your taunts and ridicule, and he creates a new hell for you to fight."

"You're lying," I said, seething.

"It's all there in Stevie's comic book. Read it for yourself."

I made a half turn toward it and stopped. "I won't. I don't need to. I know it's not true."

The Délon groaned. "Well, aren't you boring?"

I raised the crossbow and pointed it at him. "Actually, you're the boring one, and I'm getting tired of this conversation. We're on a tight schedule."

"I know," the Délon said. "To save Gordy. To find Lou. To blah, blah, blah. It's always the same with you, isn't it, son?"

I fired the crossbow and severed one of his spider hair locks. The dead-eyed freak screeched and came close to dropping Minnow. "I told you not to call me that."

"You shouldn't test my patience!"

I reloaded the crossbow. "You can skip the tough talk. I know how weak you are. The cold almost killed you, and the heat from these fires isn't enough to get you back to full strength. Without something to eat, you'll be dead in a day, maybe two."

He snickered. “What a smart boy you are. You are right. Indeed you are, but you’ve made a terrible assumption.”

“What’s that?”

“That I didn’t pack a lunch.” He grinned, and I could feel my pulse in my neck flutter. “Lunch, get out here!”

A thin, frail man came out from behind a row of shelving in the front of the store. His clothes were hanging off of him, and I could hear his flat bare feet slap against the floor as he approached.

“Tell the boy… Excuse me, the man, tell him your name, lunch.”

The thin man looked my way. His pupils appeared as if they were struggling to hold up his eyelids. In a soft, weak voice he said, “My name is lunch.”

The Délon laughed that horrible Délon laugh. “He’s trained so well. Tell Oz your real name.”

Lunch’s mouth hung open, and he closed his eyes. After several seconds he fought to open them. “My name is Blake, Tyler Blake.”

The Délon sniffed the air. “Tyler is afraid, aren’t you, Tyler?”

The thin man nodded.

“The fear gives his blood a bit of a spicy taste. Perfect for this excursion into the cold. But, Tyler is hopeful, too. That hope is so, so sweet. The sweetness relieves the stress. It’s really a perfect combination.”

Tyrone furrowed his brow. “He doesn’t look very hopeful.”

The Délon snapped. “Are you calling me a liar? Tell our visitors you’re hopeful, lunch!”

Tyler swallowed the moist air. “I’m hopeful.”

"For what?" I asked.

He stared at me for a few seconds and then said, "I'm hopeful I'll die soon." Tears streamed down his cheek.

I raised the crossbow and shot Tyler between the eyes. The room exploded with reactions. All of them directed at me. All of them centered on one emotion: anger. The Délon was angry I had killed his food source. The others were angry I had killed an innocent man. They yelled and growled and looked at me as if I had lost my mind. I hadn't. Killing Tyler Blake was the sanest, kindest thing I had ever done. I had seen his eyes. Even though I had never known him, the man he used to be was forever gone. For as long as he lived, he would know nothing but terror and anguish. I didn't kill an innocent man. I killed a man who had died a long, long time ago.

By the time I reloaded my crossbow, I started to doubt myself. If I had my choice, I would have fallen to my knees and bawled my eyes out. I would have punched the floor until I had broken every bone in my hand. I would have curled up in a ball and sobbed until I stopped breathing.

But I didn't have a choice. I had to be a Creyshaw. I had people to fight and die for. There was no time to second guess myself. I couldn't afford to look weak and unsure. I had to keep moving forward in this brutal place like a savage doing whatever it takes to beat back the monsters that wanted to see us all suffer and die.

The Délon was so shocked by what I had done he loosened his grip on Minnow just enough for the little Ninja was to work himself free.

Ariabod hesitated long enough to ensure the boy was clear before he leapt on the Délon's back and sank his teeth into the purple freak's shoulder. The Délon flailed about and rammed the gorilla into a row of glass freezer doors on the back wall. Ariabod refused to let go.

I aimed my crossbow but couldn't find a shot.

Ajax moved in and swept the Destroyer's leg. Both he and Ariabod fell to the floor, causing the building to shake and snow to rain down on the floors from the holes in the ceiling. Ariadbod was momentarily stunned, but he never lost his grip on the Délon. Together, he and Ajax were able to immobilize the giant dead-eyed monster.

I instructed Tyrone to hold Minnow back , and I approached the gorillas and the Délon with my crossbow aimed and ready to fire.

The Délon stopped struggling when he saw me. "You are feeble, human."

"That's funny. This human is about to end you, Délon."

"You can end me, but you can't end us! We are meant to rule!"

"Rule what? A rotten, dying planet?"

He groaned. "Kill me and be done with it. I no longer have an interest in doing what I was sent here to do."

I applied pressure to the trigger but quickly eased up. "What were you sent here to do?"

"Just kill him, Oz!" Tyrone shouted.

"Yes, just kill me!"

"What were you sent here to do?"

"To make you a deal."

I shook my head. "I'm tired of deals. The Pure, The Gore, every ugly thing in this world always wants to make deals with me."

"Then kill me!"

I took care to aim.

"What do I care if you get your precious Lou?" the Délon said.

I smiled. "We can get her back without your help."

"I'm not talking about getting her back, you idiot. I'm talking about getting your Lou as you want her."

I pointed the crossbow up and off of him. "As I want her? What does that mean?"

"Real."

The word bounced around in my head before I could really grasp onto what he was saying. When it sank in, my hands started to shake. I dropped the crossbow to my side in an effort to conceal how unnerved I was by what he said.

"That's what you want, isn't it? You want Lou to be real so if you find a way back she can go with you."

"You're lying."

He grinned. "I'm not. We can make her real."

"The Pure said it can't be done…"

"The Pure is no longer in command for a reason, my boy. He lacks imagination. General Roy has solved your dilemma. He's found a way to make Lou real."

I didn't respond right away. I didn't know if I wanted to hear anymore. Half of my brain was telling me he was lying, trying to trick me to save his own neck, but the other half was open to the idea that he was telling the truth. "How?"

"We are in possession of the thing that controls all that is real and unreal in this world. Remember?" He hesitated and then added. "It is more accurate to say that we are in partial possession of…"

"The Storytellers?" I snapped.

He snapped back, "Storytellers!"

He raised his voice so loudly that a ringing hiss filled the small store.

"Their minds created this world. They can change it as we see fit. They put me here, didn't they? We hold four of the Storytellers… "

I shook my head. "You must think I'm a fool. If they could change it, you would have had them do it by now. There would be no war. I wouldn't be here if you could have the Storytellers change things as you see fit." I raised my crossbow once again.

"Four Storytellers do not have the strength. Not to make meaningful changes. They can do small things, yes, like giving a Délon the strength to survive the cold long enough to find shelter, a shelter that came equipped with burning garbage cans for heat."

I scanned the flames and turned back to him. "So, you're telling me you don't have a way to make Lou real."

"I'm telling you, that we, you and the Délons have a way. You can give us a fifth Storyteller."

"I don't have…" I started, but stopped when I realized what he was saying. "Nate?"

"He is the most powerful of all, Oz. He has been trained well by his Keeper. You bring him to us, and we can give you Lou, real, able to live in this world and yours."

"We're never making it back to our world," I said. "It doesn't make any difference if Lou is real or not."

He groaned. "You humans are so thick-headed and stupid. If the Storytellers can make a girl real, they can send you home, all of you. They can split our two worlds."

"It's a trick, Oz," Tyrone said. "He just wants to get his hands on Nate."

The Délon groaned. "You idiotic boy! I cannot leave this place. I am done no matter Oz's decision. I have no reason to lie."

"This is a suicide mission?" I asked.

"It is," he answered. "I give my life so Délons rule once again. As it should be."

I set the crossbow on the floor.

"Oz, what are you doing? You're not considering his deal, are you?" Tyrone asked.

The Délon smiled. "Of course he is. It is the only thing that makes sense."

I walked to the front door of the store and pushed the door open. The awnings over the gas pumps left a large open area in front of the building. It was an icy cathedral.

"It doesn't make sense. You can't give them Nate. This will all have been for nothing. Everyone who died..."

"Bring him out here," I said to the gorillas.

The Délon was frightened. "What are you doing?"

"I'm speeding up your suicide mission."

The gorillas dragged him across the floor. "You can't. The girl, she'll be as you want her. You will go home. All will be as it once was. It's in the comic book. The one on the counter. It just requires Nate's final touches. The last pages."

I ran to the counter and picked up the comic book.

"Read it! It will show the way. It has the answers. It will show you how to take Nate from his Keeper and end all this."

I held the comic book in my hand and stared at it. The thought entered my head. *This could all be over.* All I had to do was give them Nate.

The Délon could see I was giving it some thought. "You know it is for the best."

I walked towards him.

"Oz, I won't let you do it," Tyrone said gripping his knife tightly.

I smiled at him and dropped the comic book into one of the flaming trash cans.

The Délon no longer put up a struggle. Ajax and Ariabod stopped at the open door. "You fool! You human piece of garbage! You idiot!"

I ran over and knelt down next to him. "I am Creyshaw, Délon. I would never betray Nate."

I stood and directed Ajax and Ariabod to drag him outside. They happily complied. The temperature dropped 40 degrees almost instantly. The Délon shook, and I could see his skin twitch.

"In the snow," I said pointing to the wall of snow at the back of the icy cathedral.

The two gorillas dragged the weakened Délon as fast as they could to the snow.

Tyrone stepped outside with me. "I almost thought you were going to…"

"You know me better than that," I said.

He looked at Tyler's dead body. "I thought I did, boss. I thought I did."

I didn't acknowledge him. Instead, I moved to the Délon who was no convulsing as he sat propped up against the cold snow.

"Hurts," he said.

"I know the feeling," I said.

"I am not like you," he said.

I heard a pop and watched as a piece of his purple skin exploded off his face. "How so?"

"I will not survive this. I cannot live as a human. Not anymore."

I sat next to him. The others reentered the store. "I know."

More of his skin cracked and fell away. His spider leg hairdo crumbled. He screamed.

I fought the urge to look at him too closely. I knew I would start to see my father. I didn't want to see that. I had already thought of my father as being dead. I didn't want to face the fact that he had only been trapped in a monster's body.

I heard a loud sizzle followed by a bang. A small explosion blew my hair to the side, and I could feel Délon skin raining down on me. I took a deep breath and turned to the slime-covered face of my father. He was struggling to breathe. Weakly, he reached out his hand for, but couldn't muster enough strength. It fell limp to his chest.

I leaned in and whispered, "I don't want to be a Creyshaw anymore, dad. I want to go home. I want to be with you and mom again. Like it used to be, only I'll be better this time. I won't disobey you. I won't be mean to Stevie. I just want to go home."

He managed a small smile. "I'm glad I got to see you all grown up. You really are a man now." He wheezed and opened his eyes wide. "I can see Kimball. Your mother..."

I looked up and only saw the gas pump awning.

He swallowed and said, "I am home." With that, my father breathed his last.

I buried my eyes into his shoulder and cried like I've never cried before. I was tired of losing my family. And they were all gone because of me. I killed them all. Just like I killed Stevie Dayton. I had done all this, and they paid for it, everyone I loved.

Once I walked back into the store, I was greeted by stares from Ajax and Tyrone. They both nodded to let me know I wasn't alone. They knew the pain I was feeling. We didn't need to talk about it. We just needed to get back to our mission, to find the Gore.

I saw the legs of Tyler Blake sticking out of from behind a row of empty shelves. I gestured toward them with my chin and said, "We have to take care of him."

Tyrone looked in that direction. "The thing is he's just like that dead guy in the emergency vehicle, isn't he?"

"What do you mean?"

Tyler shrugged, "I mean he's dead, too, and we were going to use the other guy as bait."

I gave his suggestion some thought. "This is different."

"How?"

"I didn't kill the guy in the truck," I said as I moved to the body.

When I rounded the shelves, I examined Tyler's face. He was so skinny I could see the outline of his teeth against his cheekbones. I scanned down and was sickened by the almost chalky white color of his skin. How the man had been able to stand was a mystery. I reached down to grab his legs, but stopped when I noticed something. His hands were missing. Standing, I yelled, "Tyrone!"

He came running.

"You took his hands?" I asked, pointing at one of the stubs.

Tyrone shook his head. "I didn't touch him."

I leaned in closer. The hands had been cut off by someone who was handy with a knife because it was a clean cut. I twirled around. "Minnow."

"That little sneak," Tyrone said.

I moved past him and quickly made my way to the other end of the store. Minnow wasn't there. I checked the opposite corner and then behind the register. "Where'd he go?"

Tyrone held up his hands. "I don't know."

"Damn!" I ran to the back office and noticed a number of sturdy grates piled on top of the desk. It was just the right height for Minnow to climb up and out of the store. I carefully climbed his makeshift ladder and poked my head through the hole. Minnow was just reaching the tree line. I almost shouted for him to stop, but quickly realized it was useless. Turning back to the front of the store, I instructed Tyrone to get the gorillas out and then burn Tyler's body. I pulled myself out of the hole before he grudgingly agreed.

Catching up to Minnow wasn't easy. He was quicker across the snow than I was because he didn't sink as far down. We were at the bottom of the small hill that led to the entrance of the courthouse before I put my hand on his shoulder and convinced him to stop.

He jerked away. I counted myself lucky he didn't pull his knife.

"What are you doing?" I asked, talking slowly and loudly.

He didn't need to hear me or be able to read my lips to see that I was upset. He quickly removed his backpack and opened it. Without hesitation, he pulled out one of Tyler's hands and showed it to me.

"Yeah, I figured that much out. You shouldn't have done that."

He stomped his foot and pointed up to the sky. Darkness was fast approaching.

"Okay, so we were running out of daylight, but you can't just do stuff like that," I said pointing at the severed hand. "Not until we talk it over."

He didn't understand a word I said. He stuffed the hand back in his pack and turned to leave.

I grabbed him by the shoulder again. "Wait!"

He groaned and gritted his teeth. After several seconds, he swallowed and talked. It was obvious it was something he didn't do very often, and the words that came out of his mouth were like no words I had heard before. Giii Looo baa kk."

I looked at him dumbfounded, and he repeated the phrase if you could call it that.

"Gii Loo baa kk."

I repeated the words to myself. Finally, I pieced it together. "Get Lou back."

He seemed satisfied that I got it right and started to turn to walk away, but I stopped him again.

Holding my hand up, I said the one thing I hoped would make him stay. "Wait for Ajax."

He nodded and sighed in relief. While we waited, I found myself happy the kid was on my side. He did something I didn't have the guts or brains to do, or rather he didn't do something. He didn't hesitate to do what had to be done.

Chapter Nineteen

When we made it back to the tunnel, we had to rest. Time was against us, but everyone of us who had traipsed through the snow and back were worn out. The cold, the thick, soft snow, the run-in with my father the Délon, and the ordeal with Tyler had made us zoned out zombies.

I found a spot on the platform away from everybody and sat down with my legs pulled into my body as close as I could get them. After placing my forehead on my knees, I managed about ten minutes of sleep before Wes woke me up by sitting next to me.

"You okay?" he asked.

I yawned and nodded.

"I heard what happened."

"Tyrone?"

"Who else? None of the others can talk."

I managed a half smile.

He leaned back and stretched out his legs. "I ever tell you I almost got married once?"

I shook my head.

"Patricia Dolan. Pretty little thing. Prettier than a fat redneck like me deserved. We dated in high school, and when we graduated, I popped the question."

"She said yes?"

"She did, but she didn't mean it. She was too young and too nice to say no, so she said yes because she thought that's what I wanted to hear. She was right. It was what I wanted to hear, but only if she meant it. She broke off the engagement about a month later and at the time it crushed me to a fine dust."

"What's your point?"

He had drifted back in his mind to his time with pretty little Patricia Dolan. "My point is during that month I spent thinking I was going to be married I started thinking about all of it. The alone time she and I would have. The house we would have. The kids, the grandkids, the life we would have."

"Alone time?"

"You know what I mean."

I snickered.

He ignored me and continued with his story. "The thing is I didn't just think about all the good that was ahead of us. The bad stuff crept into my head, too. I guess 'cause I'd grown up with a lot of bad stuff. I imagined having a son someday. I imagined all the things I would do to make sure he was safe, but I knew the world was bigger than me. I knew he was in for some bad days. It couldn't be helped. We all gotta go through it. The lucky ones survive and come out better for it."

He turned away from me, and he cleared his throat.

"Looking back, the day Patricia broke up with me was just about the best day of my life because I couldn't stop thinking about our imaginary son coming up against evil and getting beat back by it. When she told me she didn't want to get married, the first thing I thought is I'll never have to live through that. I'll never have to face it.

"I never counted on any of this. I never thought I'd be the lone adult to a bunch of rug rats. You see what I'm saying? I didn't get out from under it, Oz. I try like hell to deny it. I try to pretend that you all are nothing more to me than fellow survivors, but damn it if you all ain't my kids, every one of you. Here I am watching you all come up against the worst evil I've ever seen." He put his arm around me. "It kills me that I can't protect you from this world, son." He choked up. "I know your own father would feel the same way. And I know he'd tell you, don't let this world dictate who you become. Don't do things because you think it needs to be done, because you think that's what leaders do. Do things because that's the way your folks raised you. Be good, Oz. Be good."

I fought back my own tears. "I'm not sure how my folks raised me, Wes. I don't remember." I put my head down. "I killed that man today because I know how he felt."

Wes squeezed the back of my neck. "We all do, Oz. We all do."

Chapter Twenty

We had to stop in a couple of spots along the way to clear debris from the emergency track. Each time we did, Vance took the opportunity to let me know how terrible I was, and that he would be glad when he and Minnow were as far away from me as possible. I didn't argue with him.

When we reached our destination, Wes said, "Section 1233. Let the games begin."

I jumped off the bed of the truck and stretched my back. Tyrone did the same. Vance stayed in the front seat of the truck, mostly out of spite. In a matter of minutes, everyone else stood next to the passenger side of the truck.

"What's the plan?" Tyrone asked.

"First, we find fresh signs of the Gore, Lou, or Floyd," I said.

Wes focused on the platform and said, "I'm afraid I found something."

I followed his eyes and saw the same dome-like shelters we had seen in the woods. Only these shelters were made out of garbage and benches and anything else that was available in the tunnels.

Vance finally got out of the truck. "A nest." He hobbled to the platform. "Damn!"

"What?" Wes asked.

Vance groaned. "It's empty!" Walking back he said, "That means one thing. It's awake. If it's awake, then it's more than likely the others are awake, too." He looked up and down the tunnel. "And we're vulnerable from both sides. This is not good. Not good at all!"

"Relax," I said. "We've got an escape route if we have to use it."

"Where?"

I pointed up at the platform, but pulled my hand back when I didn't see what I assumed would be there. Every other platform we had passed had had a door marked "Surface," but unfortunately, this one didn't.

"You see what they did, don't you?" Vance asked. "The lured us into a trap."

"Hold on," Wes said. "Let's not get ahead of ourselves. All we got is one empty nest. That does not prove they lured us into a trap."

Tyrone moved to the back of the truck to get a bottle of water. He was mid-swallow when he said, "I think that might be proof they lured us into a trap."

We all looked in the direction he was staring. Dozens of Gore approached.

"Ear plugs!" Vance shouted.

We all dug through our pockets and quickly pulled out ear plugs. We stuffed them in our ear canals, and I immediately felt my pulse pounding against the foam plugs.

"Arm yourselves!" Wes screamed.

Minnow tapped me on my arm and pointed towards the other end of the tunnel. Dozens more Gore approached. This time they were led by the slight figure of a girl.

"Lou," I said to myself. Even though she was accompanied by a herd of body-part beasts, I was thrilled to see her. I wanted to go to her and plant a kiss square on her lips.

"Make sure you don't kill someone we know," I shouted in order to be heard through the every one's protected ears.

"Roger that," Wes said. "Unless it's Floyd!"

"Not even Floyd. If Gordy isn't here, he'll know how to find him. We need Floyd alive."

Vance snapped his head from one end of the tunnel to the next. "Fellas, this is crazy! We are seriously outgunned!"

"For now," I said, "But I've been down this road before! I know an out!"

"You do?" Wes asked.

I nodded.

"Well, what are you waiting for? Use it!" Vance shouted.

"Not until I have Lou, and I at least know where Gordy is!"

The Gore on either side of us kept approaching. When the first line of them stepped past the narrow tunnel and entered the open area, they stopped and swayed in unison. From a distance, it would have looked like a dance troupe getting ready to breakout into a routine. A low rumbling was coming out of their mouths. It almost sounded as if they were chanting something.

Lou broke from the Gore and kept walking until she stood ten feet away from us.

"Lou," I said.

"You shouldn't have come after me," she said with a shaky voice. She was trembling.

"We had to, sweetie," Wes said.

"I serve the Gore now!" She pointed to her ear. "No need for the plugs. There are no enchanters."

"Enchanters?" Wes asked.

She struggled to say, "Baby-heads."

I hesitated and then reached my hand up to remove an earplug. Vance stopped me.

"Don't do that, boy. She's lying."

She rolled her eyes. "They don't want you to offer yourselves to them."

"Why?" Tyrone asked. "What's wrong with us?"

She didn't answer.

"It's us," Vance said. "Me and the boy. We are their sworn enemy. Anyone that travels with us is their sworn enemy, too…"

"You flatter yourself, Vance. You are only their enemy… our enemy because you are with Minnow."

Wes shivered. "You're breaking my heart, little girl."

She glared at Wes. "Then you are a fool. Because I'm neither little nor a girl. I'm not even human."

"Listen," I said. "They've brainwashed you. One of the baby-heads…"

"I serve the Gore," she said. "It doesn't matter why or how."

"You belong with us," I said.

"It's no use," Vance said. "She's gone."

Lou looked past me and focused on Vance. "It's not too late to offer the rest of yourself, Vance. I can talk to the president. You can join us without the terror."

He pointed at his right ear to indicate the earplug. "I'm keeping mine in, so I can't hear you too well, honey. You'll have to speak up."

Back to me, Lou said, "I know he's lied to you about them. They are not what he says."

I raised an eyebrow. "We had a run in with them. We know exactly what they are."

"You don't know!" she shouted. "You judge them by their appearance. You don't see them for who they really are. They are us, Oz."

"Listen to yourself, Lou. This isn't you. You are on our side."

"I serve the Gore."

Minnow stepped out next to Ajax and drew Lou's attention away from me.

She signed to him.

Whatever she said angered Ajax. He lurched forward, barked, and slammed the floor of the tunnel with his fists.

"You keep your eyes off that boy," Vance said.

She smiled. "Why do you protect him? You know what he is."

Vance sneered at her. "I know what you are. I don't give anything you say much credence. You're a lying, thieving, murdering little girl that I should have killed the day we met."

I turned to him with enough anger in me to turn Délon. I barely managed to hold myself back. "You shouldn't talk about her like that."

The expression on his face suggested he knew it was wise not to push me any further. He simply nodded and cast his eyes to the ground.

Tyrone stepped between us. "There's no time for this, boss."

I seethed a bit longer and then returned my attention to Lou. Holding onto the tail end of my anger, I said, "You and Gordy are coming with us. Now!"

She smiled. "Still pretending to be a leader, I see."

I stepped forward. "I am the leader."

"No, you're not. A leader would never have come after me. I'm nothing, Oz. I don't belong in your world. Coming after me is useless. The way home is in Tullahoma. You know it is."

I gritted my teeth. "You are my home, you stupid idiot!"

She was taken aback. "That… that… doesn't even make sense."

I shook my head and groaned. There was so much I wanted to say to her, but it all sounded so pointless and stupid in my head.

Wes groaned louder than me. "Oh for crap sake, would you tell her how you really feel about her! Just tell her! We're all going to probably die anyway, and you might knock some sense into that clouded head of hers!"

"She knows how I feel," I said.

"She doesn't even know how she feels," Wes said. "She just knows what the Gore tells her to feel."

"I serve the Gore…"

I hurried forward and grabbed Lou by the arms. "Shut up! Shut up! Don't say that. You don't serve the Gore. You are one of us. You are real. I don't care what anyone says, even the Storytellers. You are real."

"I'm not…"

"How I feel about you is real, Lou. Don't you see? That's real. Nothing else matters. Not where you came from. Not where I came from. All that matters is how we feel about each other. I love you, Lou!"

I felt her relax for a split second. She turned her eyes up to mine and studied them. "I love…" She looked away and growled. "I am not real! If I was real, I'd be a part of the Gore. I wouldn't just serve them. I would be the Gore. They can't take body parts from a made-up girl. You can't love a made-up girl! I am a made-up girl!"

"Enough!" A voice barked out from the group of Gore behind her. The monsters stepped aside as a one of them from the back moved forward. It was taller than the others. It didn't move with an awkward gait. It was made in the same patchwork fashion as the others, but its parts seemed to be newer and more carefully fitted. The head was that of a middle-aged man, its hair was neat and styled, and with just a touch of gray on the sides.

Lou bowed down as it approached.

"This talk is getting us nowhere," the Gore said.

Wes raised his crossbow. "Don't come any closer."

"You may discharge your weapon if you wish. It cannot harm me, not permanently."

"You mind telling me how you can talk?" Wes asked. "I mean really talk."

"You mean think?" the approaching Gore asked.

"They call him the president," Lou said.

"He must be the main freak in charge," Vance said.

The talking Gore came to a stop next to Lou. "You needn't be insulting."

"Needn't I?" Vance said. "You're disgusting, you puke! I've seen what your kind does to my kind. Insulting is about the nicest thing I can be to you."

"We offer your kind a chance to belong. We are the Gore. We are all part of one another. All that is required to join us is to give yourself to us, piece by piece."

"You filthy..."

"Okay, this isn't really getting us anywhere," I said.

The Gore looked at me. "You are the president of your kind?"

I shook my head and fumbled around for a way to describe myself. Finally, I just said, "I'm more or less the head freak in charge."

"The one called Oz?"

I nodded feeling uneasy that he knew my name.

"Lou speaks of you. As does the one called Gordy."

Wes fumed, "Where is he?"

"His location is unimportant."

Wes fired his crossbow and hit the talking Gore in the shoulder. "Where is he?"

The president didn't even flinch. Without touching it, he slowly pushed the arrow out of his flesh. After it hit the ground, the president bent down and picked it up. "I am sorry you have resorted to violence."

I turned to Minnow. "Give me the hands."

He looked at me trying to figure out what I was saying to him. I wrapped my right thumb and middle finger around my wrist and shook my hand. "The hands! The hands! Give them to me."

Finally understanding what I was asking of him, he quickly removed his backpack and retrieved the hands.

I took them and showed them to the president. "I'm told the Gore prize hands."

The talking Gore's eyes lit up. "We do, yes. More than anything."

"I have two fresh hands," I said, making myself sick by referring to them as fresh. "They're yours."

He reached for them, but I pulled back.

"I want something for them."

He chuckled. "You have not properly assessed the situation, leader Oz. We, the Gore, outnumber you in overwhelming fashion."

It was my turn to chuckle. "There are more of us you cannot see."

He looked perplexed.

A quick scan of the others in my group told me they were just as confused as the talking Gore.

The president turned to Lou. "Does he tell the truth?"

Lou carefully examined my face. "I don't know of any others in his group, but I have not been with them for many, many weeks."

"There are others," I said. "They have two names. We call them Greasywhoppers and their numbers are far greater than yours."

Wes pulled me back. He whispered, "Have you gone nuts, boy? We got enough on our hands contending with the Gore. We don't need to pile on more monsters to fight."

"Trust me," I said. "I've done this kind of thing before."

"What the devil are you talking about?"

"I never would have freed you and the others without a little help from some overgrown earthworms."

He slowly nodded.

"The Ta…" Lou started to say, but stopped herself. "The Greasywhoppers are harmless now."

"You're forgetting the Walmart," Tyrone said.

"That was a glitch, a hiccup because the Délons were losing control," Lou said.

"They've lost total control," I said. "There's an all out war among the Destroyers down south."

"It's true," Tyrone added.

She hesitated. "Okay, maybe they have, but that doesn't mean the Greasywhoppers will fight for you."

"No," I said, "but if we call them out, they'll be on the hunt for us. You can bet on it. And they're going to cause a lot of pain and destruction looking for us."

Lou considered this new information and then nodded. "They're telling the truth."

The Gore president studied Lou. "Are you sure you're not lying for your old friends?"

"I serve the Gore," Lou said sounding hurt.

He reached out and gently touched her cheek with his large hands. "Of course you do." Returning his attention to me, he said, "I can give you the troublesome one for the hands."

I shook my head. "No. Two hands for two of our people."

"It is far from a fair trade." He gave a half smile.

"It's the only trade I'm offering."

A snicker escaped his putrid mouth. "It is also a trade that I cannot give because it is not mine to give."

"What are you talking about?"

"Tell them, Lou."

She avoided eye contact with me. "I serve the Gore. I won't go with you."

"You will!" I shouted.

The president laughed. "Only the death of her enchanter can sever her from service."

"Her enchanter?" I said. "The baby-head? You know where it is?"

"I know were all my constituents are, leader Oz."

"Where is it?"

The talking Gore looked at me with a furrowed brow. "What a useless question. I would never betray one of my own in such a way… not without anything in return."

I held up the hands. "The hands. It's all I have…" I stopped when my eye caught my own hands. "And mine, you can have my hands."

"Oz!" Wes shouted.

I ignored him. "You give us Gordy, Lou, and her enchanter, and I'll give you both sets of hands. You can have my legs, too. Whatever you want. Just let Lou go. Please, just let her go."

"You have lost your mind," Wes said.

"That is a tempting offer," the president said.

"No," Lou said. "I serve the Gore…"

"We already have a servant, and we can find others, but Oz the leader could be a most valuable addition to the Gore."

"I'm valuable…"Lou started.

"You are valuable to no one," the president said scornfully. "You are a useless unreal girl. We can use no part of you."

Lou shook with anger and sorrow.

"You see what you serve, Lou. They don't even appreciate what you do for them," I said.

The president tried to give her a reassuring smile. "We do indeed appreciate her. We just don't need her."

"Then you'll take the trade?"

"No, he won't," Wes said.

"But I will. On behalf of all the Gore, I will indeed."

"You ain't getting Minnow," Vance said.

The president studied the boy. "Not today, but tomorrow perhaps, or the next day. Once Oz has taken his places among us, he can help us sort out when and how."

"I'm telling you this ain't gonna happen. Oz won't be joining you," Wes said.

I patted him on the shoulder. "You're finally going to be in charge."

He choked on his words as he tried to protest.

I handed over my arrows and crossbow to Tyrone. "Never understood why you always use a knife. Try this from now on. You'll live longer."

"What are you doing?" Tyrone asked.

I knelt down to get eye to eye with Ajax. "I should have paid more attention to that whole sign language stuff, buddy." I placed my hand on his pointy head. "Get everyone home."

"This is just all nonsense," Wes said. "There ain't a chance in hell I'm going to let you go with them."

I stood and turned to the president. "What now?"

He placed his hand on Lou's cheek. "You are no longer required to serve the Gore."

Lou's face flushed red. She screamed and fell to her knees.

I bent down and put my arm around her. Whispering in her ear, I said, "You are not useless, Lou. I haven't been able to breathe without you."

She looked at me with her eyes full of tears. "I want to serve the Gore. Why can't you leave me alone so I can serve the Gore?"

I smiled at her and stood. "Where's Gordy, and Lou's enchanter?"

The president motioned to the Gore standing behind him with a simple head nod. Within minutes, Gordy was dragged through the group of monsters by the smaller Gore that had abducted him.

"Let me go, you pile of crap!"

The president sneered. "He is an endless source of frustration. I'm happy to be rid of him."

"Hey," Gordy yelled. "Y'all are here! You're really here!"

The small Gore shoved him forward.

Gordy didn't realize he was free of the monster's grip at first, but when he finally realized it, he took off in a dead sprint to us. "I can't believe it. Y'all actually came to get me." He hugged Wes.

"The enchanter?" I asked.

"That will require some time. I will have to send for it."

Wes pried himself loose from Gordy. "Then that's that. No deal."

I stared at the president. "The Gore aren't the type to lie are they?"

The president was genuinely surprised. "We have no need to lie."

"You'll stick to the deal if I go with you now?"

"We will."

"What?" Wes said sharply. "This is nuts."

"This is happening, Wes," I said sternly.

He growled. "You can't trust him, boy. He calls himself the president for Pete's sake."

"So," I said.

"I ain't known a president that didn't lie every time he opened his mouth."

The talking Gore smiled. "It does not really matter how you regard me. You are in a situation where you have very little choice. As a good leader does, Oz has found a solution that spares your life. You would be wise not to fight him on it."

I nodded. "He's right, and he's not lying." I wrapped Wes up in a hug and whispered. "I'm the one that's lying."

I released him and winked.

He furrowed his brow and said, "I sure wish I knew how that head of yours worked most of the time."

I scooped up Lou by her arm. She screamed and tried to jerk away, but I was able to push her toward Ariabod, and he easily held on to her.

The president was pleased. "You will make a fine addition, leader Oz. If all goes well, you may even serve as my second in command."

"Which part of me?" I asked nervously.

He placed his hand on my back and guided me to the Gore at the north end of the tunnel. "The head, of course. The heart, too. Your hands will be awarded to a worthy Gore. You will not be disappointed."

"Why can't I just keep what I've got and save everyone a lot of trouble."

He sounded like a school teacher trying to explain to a second grader how to do basic arithmetic when he answered. "Oh, no, no, leader Oz. The Gore must be connected. You will be divided into the smallest workable parts in order to share as much of you with as many Gore as we can. It binds us and makes us strong.

You will be so pleased to be a part of so many yet feeling one with all."

"Can't wait," I said as we moved through the Gore. They all stared at my hands. Some of them were literally drooling at the sight of them. I found myself getting ill as we headed down the tunnel. The community of Gore followed, still giving off that low rumbling chant. Finally, I said, "Do they have to do that?"

"It is their way of feeling even more connected with one another. You will see, leader Oz, that we will do anything to sustain our union."

"It's just so annoying," I said.

The president looked over his shoulder at the chanting Gore. "I find it soothing. It warms me to know my Gore brothers are so close by. You'll know the feeling soon enough."

We walked for another mile or so before we came to a large hole in the side of the tunnel. The president motioned for me to lead the way. It wasn't my preference, but I didn't have much of a choice. I climbed through the hole and entered a slightly narrower tunnel. By the smell, it must have been a sewer line.

As the tunnel got smaller and smaller, I wondered how in the world the Gore were able to fit in a space that was barely big enough for me. It was too dark for me to even see if they were still behind me. I wished I had brought some glow sticks.

I jumped when I felt something brush my leg. Looking down, I saw the dark shape of small animals scurrying around. They appeared to be carrying food in the direction we were headed.

"You sure this was a good Idea?" I asked the president.

Several seonds passed before he answered, and somehow his voice came from in front of me. "You needn't worry, leader Oz."

I saw a dim light ahead and picked up my pace. I had to stoop so I didn't hit my head as I got closer I got to the light. It felt like the world was closing in on me. I was reminded of the cave where a Shunter has sucked on my brain.

I was almost through the hole before I even realized what it was. I was entering a utility room of some sort. Pipes of various sizes crisscrossed the ceiling and the walls were moldy and damp. I looked back in the direction I had come to see how the Gore could have possibly followed me. I was sorry I did.

The small animals weren't animals at all. They were the hands of the Gore carrying the various body parts through the narrow tunnel. They assembled the president first, and they did it impossibly fast. An army of hands put the talking Gore together in no more than 15 seconds. It was amazing and frightening to witness.

When the president was assembled, they broke off into smaller groups and started reassembling other Gore three by three.

"Where is this enchanter?" I asked.

"Not far," the president said. "You will be taken to him."

I heard a door slam above my head followed by the sound of someone quickly descending a metal staircase. I watched as Floyd made his way down the last set of stairs

"What's he doing here?" Floyd asked.

"Ah, Chef Floyd," the president said with great affection for his human servant, "Leader Oz has volunteered to join the Gore. Aren't you so pleased?"

Floyd looked me up and down. "What's your angle?"

I paused before answering him because I had to fight the urge to grab him by the throat and snap his neck. "We made a deal."

"Deal?"

"One that benefits us all," the president said.

Floyd scanned the dank room and then asked in a panic, "Where's Lou?"

The president moved to a large cement box in the middle of the room. "Leader Oz has exchanged himself for the useless girl." He pushed back the top of the box just enough for him to reach his furry, bulky arm inside.

"Exchanged?" Floyd barked. "No, no, tha-tha-that's not going to work for me! I asked you if Lou could help me, and you said yes. Now-now-now you want to take her away from me. I need Lou. You have to get her back."

The president pulled a fat raccoon out of the box, and held it by the tail. The animal screeched and twisted about. "I cannot."

"Why?"

"Because as leader Oz has said, we have made a deal. I cannot bring Lou back because that would nullify our deal."

"But-but-but you said the deal benefited us all. It doesn't benefit me. Lou was for me. You said I could have her. That was the deal you made with me."

The president considered Floyd's statement with the raccoon still squirming in his hand. "I had not considered our agreement a deal."

"It was. Just as much a deal as the deal you made with Oz. You can't go back on a deal."

The president grabbed the raccoon with his other hand and with a quick jerk he tore the animal in half. I turned away, but not before I saw blood spray out in every direction. "I'm afraid I did not make our arrangement clear, Chef Floyd. We do not have a deal. You serve the Gore at our pleasure and in return we allow you to belong even though there is no place for you in our community. Do you no longer wish to belong with us, Chef Floyd?"

Floyd hesitated. "I do. I do. I just... Lou was like me. We were a team." He stopped to wipe the snot running from his nose. "I-I-I... she was my friend."

The president bit into the raccoon's intestines after he said, "We'll find you a new friend. One who will serve the Gore with as much dedication as you this time. The girl was far too argumentative for my liking."

"But she was my friend," Floyd repeated sounding more than betrayed by the Gore he served.

"You've made that point," The president said ripping a limb from the raccoon and handing it to a nearby Gore. The grotesque beast devoured it in record time. "The girl is not even here, and she is a cause for grief. I am glad to be rid of her."

"Can we get an ETA on the enchanter? I'll feel a lot better when that part of our deal is taken care of," I said.

The president smiled. "You are so anxious to join the Gore. I am pleased. Floyd, see to it that Lou's enchanter is making haste our way."

Floyd was confused. "What do you want with Lou's enchanter?"

"I tire of explaining myself to you," the president said. "You were never this difficult before the girl arrived."

"Part of the deal," I said jumping in.

"What would you want with the enchanter?" Floyd asked.

"What do you think?" I said. "I want to release Lou from her service to the Gore."

Floyd's complexion turned ghostly white. "No! I won't allow it! She serves the Gore. She served you well, Mr. President. Did she not?"

He rolled his eyes. "She was adequate. I am confident we can find a better servant."

Floyd roared in anger. The echo from his mad howl bounced all around the room.

The president rushed him and grabbed Floyd up by his ear, causing the chef to now howl in pain. "I could tear you apart without effort. Is that what you wish I do?"

Floyd struggled to speak through the pain. "Do it! Make me a part of the Gore! I want to be part of you!"

The president tossed Floyd to the ground. "You know that cannot be, yet you insist on wasting our time by making the request over and over again."

Floyd sobbed. "You don't know what it's like."

"I don't wish to hear this again. I know your sorrows by heart. You are unwanted. You are unloved. You are so alone and lost and unhappy. Your endless misery is of no interest to me. It is of no interest to anyone because you have no kind..."

"Lou is my kind, but you sent her away..."

"You are a broken record!" The president stood over Floyd, barely able to contain his rage.

"I'm sorry. I'm sorry. I'm sorry."

"You see the pointless drivel we must put up with from such unwanted trash?" the president asked me.

I went from hating Floyd to feeling sorry for him. But I didn't want to let on that I was having second thoughts about the deal I had made with the Gore, so I simply said, "I see, yes."

"I've given him a purpose, yet it is not enough."

"It is," Floyd said cowering with his hands up to protect himself from the expected beating.

Instead, the president gently patted his servant on the shoulder. "You have been our most worthy servant so far, Chef Floyd. Why do you invite these angry outbursts from me?"

Floyd sobbed even harder. "I'm not worthy. I'm not."

"Here, stand," the president said helping Floyd to his feet. "Let us consider this a misunderstanding between associates."

Floyd forced a smile and nodded nervously. "Yes, a misunderstanding. One that I initiated. I am your humble servant, Mr. President. I serve all the Gore with humility and gratitude."

The president took Floyd's face in his hands. "And leader Oz will be part of us soon. Once we have taken care of this business with Lou's enchanter, I want you to prepare our newest convert to be assembled in a way that is fitting for my second in command."

"Second in command?" Floyd asked, looking in my direction.

"He has much to offer. His heart and mind shall remain united."

"Heart and mind?" I said. "That's why you can think? Your heart and brain came from the same..."

"Human?" The president said as he approached. "It is indeed why I can think. It is a right of assembly that is reserved for the Gore leadership. You should be honored to be granted this right. There are only a handful of such assembled among the Gore."

"I don't understand," I said. "Why not grant every Gore this right of assembly?"

He looked at me as if I had lost my mind. "The Gore cannot function with hordes of free thinkers. Such a privilege is granted to the smallest number of individuals possible. It is the only way to maintain order and live in a unified manner."

Floyd finally pulled himself together enough to stand. Brushing himself off, he asked, "Shall I take leader Oz to the enchanter now?"

"Yes, do, and hurry. I'm anxious to fulfill our deal so he can join us."

Floyd put on a fake smile and invited me to go ahead of him up the metal staircase. I made the climb as the president continued munching on his fresh raccoon kill. The other Gore gathered around him and clamored for a taste of the meat.

At the top of the stairs, there was a door that opened up into an empty parking garage. "Where are we?" I asked, feeling the chill of a sudden drop in temperature.

Floyd snapped, "I don't know! I'm not a travel agent!"

"Is there a problem?" I asked.

"Is there a problem?" he repeated. His face was blood red from holding back his rage. "You ruined my life!"

I almost laughed. "I ruined your life? You're kidding, right?"

"I had everything!"

"Everything?"

"I had somewhere I belonged! I had a purpose! I had a friend!"

I shrugged my shoulders. "You still have someplace where you belong, and you still have a purpose."

"But I don't have Lou!"

This time I let myself laugh. "You never had Lou!"

He rushed me, but I stepped to the side and he tumbled to the cement floor of the garage. He had difficulty regaining his footing. "Lou is mine! She's like me! Don't you get it? We belong together!"

"Like you? You keep saying that. What does it mean?"

"It means I'm like her. We're like each other. What don't you understand about that?"

I furrowed my brow. "Are you saying you're not real?"

He threw up his hands. "Oh my God! Yes! I thought I was going to have to spell it out for you! You really are dense, you know it? I can't see why the president wants you to be part of the leadership."

I scanned him up and down. "How do you know you're not real?"

"The Gore. They wouldn't take me. They have a sense about these things. They know about me. They know about Lou. They can't use our parts because our parts aren't real."

I wanted to feel bad for him, but I couldn't manage it. "That's a sad story, but just because you're not real doesn't make you anything like Lou. Now, take me to the enchanter."

He snickered. "You know nothing about Lou."

"I've known her since I was 13. I'd say I know her a hell of a lot better than you do."

He put his finger in my face, and I was tempted to grab it and twist it until I heard it pop. "That Lou doesn't exist anymore. She vanished the day she found what she truly was." He put his hands on his hips and tilted his head from side to side as he studied my face. "No, before that. She vanished the day you found out what she truly was."

I shoved him back. "You don't know what you're talking about."

"Admit it," he said as he prepared for me to rush him. "You see her differently. She's not the Lou you thought she was."

I gritted my teeth. "Take me to the enchanter."

"She's a fake, useless girl that came from nowhere."

I used all my willpower to stay put, but it did not stop me from giving him a hateful glare. "Do you want me to kill you?"

"No, I want you to go away! Leave! Run back to your people!"

"Not without the enchanter's head."

"But you can't have it," he said sounding as if he were about to drop to his knees and beg. "You can't. She won't come back if you destroy the enchanter's head. She has to come back. I cannot bear it if she doesn't come back."

I worked to steady my anger. "You care about her?"

"She is my friend." He sighed deeply. "My only friend. My first friend. I care more about her than I care about myself."

"Then you should be helping me."

He waved me off.

"Help me release her from her service to the Gore."

He smirked. "Have you not heard a word I've said? She must stay with me. We both must serve the Gore. It is what we were meant to do. It is why we were created."

"No, it wasn't. It can't be."

"Then why are we here?"

I searched and searched for an answer that would make him happy.

"You don't know..."

"Okay, so I don't know why you're here. But I do know why Lou is here, and it's not to serve the Gore."

He grumbled turned his back on me.

"I'm not even sure why we're arguing about this. The president has ordered you to take me to the enchanter. The deal has been made."

He didn't acknowledge what I had said.

"Floyd, do what your precious Gore leader told you to do and take me to Lou's enchanter."

He shook his head.

"You don't have a choice."

He quickly whirled around holding a large kitchen knife. "I could kill you. Say it was an accident. You jumped me. I stabbed you through the heart. He'd understand. He'd have to."

My eyes dropped to the gleaming steel of the knife and noticed that he was shaking. I stepped toward him. "Do it then."

He bit his bottom lip and did a half thrust forward with the knife and then barked out in pain. His grip loosed, and the knife fell to the floor.

"You can't hurt me, can you? You want to cut my heart out, but you can't. The Gore won't let you."

He let out another howl. "I serve the Gore!"

"And when you try not to?"

"My joints burn and my muscles cramp! It is agony!"

"So, that settles it. Take me to the enchanter."

He was exhausted from the sudden charge of pain. Breathing heavily he nodded and slowly headed for a ramp leading to the upper levels of the garage. "What I'm feeling," he said. "The pain?"

"What about it?"

"Because of you, Lou is feeling it, too."

I stopped following him. "What do you mean?"

"I mean you are preventing her from serving the Gore. The longer she is away, the worse the pain will get." When he realized I was no longer following him, he turned to me and smiled. "If you cared for her, you would let her go and end her agony."

Chapter Twenty-One

I'm not sure what it was about the earplugs that prevented the enchanter from working its magic on me, but the second Floyd said the baby-head Gore was near, I stuffed my ears with the squishy nubs. I could still hear the beast coo and cry, but as long as I kept a little distance between the enchanter and me, the earplugs muffled its sounds just enough not to have an effect on me.

"The president wishes you to travel faster," Floyd said to the Gore. "You've been called to sacrifice for all Gore-kind."

The enchanter clapped its small hands and a smile spread across its chubby, decaying cheeks.

"It's happy about dying?" I asked.

"No," Floyd said. "The enchanter is honored to be called to sacrifice for the Gore."

We stood on a street of a town I did not know. The wind blew in all directions, and icy snow came at us like bullets. We hurried into a nearby building to escape the stinging cold.

Standing in the lobby of an office for a real estate company, I stared in horror at the baby-head Gore, and found myself hating it and feeling sorry for it at the same time.

Floyd snickered when he saw the expression on my face. "You judge what you don't understand."

"You think I don't understand the Gore? I get it. I've been fighting monsters since I woke up in this twisted world."

"The Gore are not monsters!" Floyd said angrily. "They are survivors, the same as me and you, for that matter.

"They may be survivors, but they're nothing like us… Well, me anyway. They may not be Destroyers, but they might as well be."

Floyd growled. "They do not destroy. They create and rebuild."

"They kill and mutilate and divide up parts of the living, and the dead," I said. "Technically, I guess they do create and rebuild, but they do it in a very twisted and sickening way."

"They do it because their way is better. You're too ignorant and stubborn to see it. But they live as one. They are connected to each other. They value one Gore as much as the next."

"Yeah? Kind of strange how they value your enchanter so much that they're going to sacrifice it for me."

"They do it for the good of the Gore. I admit I don't see it, but the president thinks your leadership can make the Gore better."

"And he's always right?"

Floyd nodded. "Even when he's wrong he's right. He created himself from the dead parts of this world. The Storytellers that Lou's always going on about, they had no hand in his creation. He took the destruction they created and built the Gore. Such a thing makes him infallible."

I watched as the enchanter shuffled mindlessly from one end of the room to the other. Leaning in, I whispered to Floyd, "I could just burn the head now and be done with it."

He looked at me like I had just insulted his mother. "That is not the way these things are done. There is a ceremony. The enchanter will be given full honors before it's terminated."

"But Lou is in agony. You said it yourself."

He bore his teeth. "That is on you, Oz."

I grabbed him by his collar. "What's to stop me from just ripping its head off and leaving?"

He laughed. "One, you don't know where we are. Two, you didn't honestly think the president would let me escort you alone, did you?'

Two large Gore with pig heads stepped out of the shadows of the lobby. I don't know how they got there, or how they could stay so well hidden, but they did not like me manhandling their servant. I let him go.

"You are under the impression that my feelings for Lou usurp my allegiance to the Gore. Nothing could be further from the truth. I love the Gore, and I would lay down my life for the president if need be. Lou is important to me but not as important as my duty to the Gore. I would even kill her to fulfill it. As she would do to me if it were necessary for her to carry out her duty to the Gore."

"You don't love the Gore."

He shook his head and tried to walk away from me.

"You've been enchanted by one of these freaky things," I said gesturing to the baby-head Gore. "That's not love. That's some kind of magic trick. It's got you under its spell."

He groaned. "What do you think love is, Oz?"

Love is something that... It makes you feel really strongly about... Love is doing what you have to..."

He chuckled. "You see?"

"No," I said, sounding frustrated. "I don't see. Love doesn't take your freewill and make you do stupid things."

"Why are you here?"

"To save Lou. To bring her home."

"But she's told me she can't go back with you."

"I'll find a way."

"But it's impossible."

"It's not."

"It is."

"No, it's not and even if it is, I have to try!"

"You have to try?" He asked.

"Yes!"

"So, it appears your love for Lou has stolen your freewill and made you do something supremely stupid like giving yourself to the Gore."

I thought long and hard about what he said. "It's not the same thing."

He rolled his eyes. "Was this your plan? To try and talk some sense into me so I'll hand over the enchanter's head, and you can run off and live happily ever after with Lou?"

I shrugged. "I'm more or less winging it at this point."

"Lou said that about you."

"What?"

"That you have an annoying habit of believing you can get yourself out of any jam, and that you also have an annoying habit of being right." He moved to the door. "I'm afraid you won't succeed this time." He pushed the door open. "We should get going. The president made it clear that he's anxious to have you join the Gore."

I stood hoping that I'd think of something before the Gore had me in pieces and handed me out like chips at a party. "I can't wait," I said sarcastically.

He shook his head. "You joke even though you know you are killing Lou."

"I'm not the one that screwed with her head and made her a servant to the Gore..."

"But you are keeping her from serving..."

"It's just temporary. As soon as we get this big, ugly baby thing to the president, it'll be history and Lou will be back to her old self."

He groaned. "You know nothing of the Gore ways. The enchanter will be sacrificed with honors. There is a ceremony. There is a feast. There is a celebration."

I considered his statement. "How long?"

"It depends on how great the sacrifice. Given that this enchanter is being sacrificed to make way for a new Gore leader, I'm guessing it could last a week or longer."

"A week?"

He grinned. "Things just got a little more complicated in Oz's world, huh?"

"What about Lou?"

"What about her?"

"She'll be in pain that whole week?"

He shook his head. "No. You don't have to worry about that. She'll be dead in three days."

I looked at him with more hatred in my heart than I thought possible.

"She won't eat. The pain will drain her. It'll be too much for her fake system. She died the second you made the deal with the president."

Chapter Twenty-Two

The president was almost giddy when we returned. He was not sure that I would keep our deal. I had proven myself worthy of not only joining the Gore, but being his second in command.

He sat in his damp room on his concrete box and watched as two of the smaller Gore entertained him by juggling various body parts. As disgusting as it was, even I had to admit they were excellent jugglers

"Leader Oz," he said, "do you know the story of the Gore?"

I didn't answer right away because I was looking for a way to get to the enchanter, snatch its head from its bulky body and escape through the small tunnel that lead to the subway system. The Gore would have to break down in smaller parts to follow me. It wasn't a perfect plan, but it had at least a chance of working.

"Oz the leader," the president repeated, "have you heard the story of the Gore, our beginning?"

"Huh?" I said. "Um, no. Can't wait to hear it."

The president stood and began his story. "It was the final night of the last real moon. The planet was on the verge of falling into a world of constant agony..."

I scanned the room for a path to the enchanter. The room was packed with Gore, and most of them were gathered around the baby-head. The monster was their hero for the sacrifice it was about to make. The others treated it like he was a soldier about to go off to war.

"... Enlivened by the cold, the hand of Kyle crawled out of the freezing, wet ground and searched for a place where it could find wisdom and strength..."

I looked at the president and prayed he wouldn't ask me to respond or participate in his story because I wasn't listening at all. It was like he was a king on his throne, a lonely king on his throne. The other Gore weren't anywhere near him now. I couldn't be sure they were even listening to his story. They were all so spellbound by the enchanter. They probably wouldn't even know if the president stopped talking. It's possible they wouldn't even know if he got up and walked out of the room.

I shifted my gaze to the enchanter. Even more of the Gore were around crowded it now. The president continued to speak, but he had no audience. It did not matter to him. I could walk right up to him, and he would barely be aware I was there. The other Gore certainly wouldn't know. I thought to myself, *too bad I don't need the president's head. I'd probably be halfway to the subway tunnel before the other Gore noticed.* I snickered to myself and then considered the idea again.

The president's head did me no good as far as Lou was concerned, but it could be useful as a bargaining chip. Surely they would hand over the enchanter's head in exchange for their beloved president's head.

I studied the activity in the room even intently. The Gore were all preoccupied, but there were a lot of them. Quickly counting four by four, there were in excess of 72 Gore, big and small. I looked up past the first flight of the metal staircase and saw Floyd glaring at me. He was paying very close attention to every move I made.

There was a way to do this. I'd have to rip the head off and go through the small tunnel, just as I'd thought of doing with the enchanter's head. But I'd have to arrange for the exchange before. I looked at my wrist. I still had Floyd's watch.

I could pull it off, I thought, *if I can get mad enough*. A little Délon assist would be just the thing I needed.

I felt my heart pump faster because I knew in my head I had already committed to the plan. Lou would be disappointed to know that I didn't always think I was right. In fact, I was pretty sure I was going to fail.

I approached the stairs with Floyd eyeballing me the whole way. Slowly, I started climbing the stairs making a point to keep my eyes down on my feet. When I reached the level Floyd was standing on, I sighed, took off the watch, and handed it to him.

He held it up. "I appreciate you taking such good care of it."

I nodded. "Do you know where the Northampton County Courthouse is?"

Putting the watch on his wrist, he said, "I may have been there a few times."

"Meet me there in 24 hours."

He cocked an eyebrow. "Meet you there? What are you talking about?"

"Bring the enchanter's head, if you want him back."

"Him? Him who?"

I didn't answer his question. "When Lou is free from service to the Gore, the first thing she'll do is kill as many of those piles of pus as she can."

His face twitched. "She wouldn't do that. She loves the Gore."

"She'll rip them apart and burn them piece by piece!"

He turned away from me. "You're just mouthing off because you like to hear yourself talk."

"I want to know what you're going to do to her after she kills some of your precious Gore."

He didn't respond.

"Tell me," I said in a whisper.

"You don't want to know," he said.

"But I do. I need to know."

He looked me over. "You need to know what? That I'll slice her belly open and pull her intestines out for the Gore to feast on! That I'll treat her like the traitor she is. That she will die an agonizing death and beg for her life and that you won't be able to do anything to stop me because you won't be you anymore. You will be the Gore. You will munch on her guts with the rest of them."

I felt a sharp pain run up my spine as the anger inside me grew. Hearing him talk about killing Lou was a good start, but I needed to be angrier if I wanted to get some of my Délon to come out. "I don't plan on joining the Gore, but if by some miracle, this goes the president's way and I'm second in command, you're history."

Now I could see the anger in his face. "I serve the Gore."

"You did serve the Gore. You're gone once I make my case to the president. You are a pathetic excuse for a servant." I was nearly nose-to-nose with him. "You love the Gore? The Gore wants nothing to do with you."

He let out a scream like a mad man and threw a fist into my jaw. I stumbled backwards and crashed down the stairs. A bolt of rage shot through me, and I knew I was there. I felt stronger. I could rip through a dozen Gore with no problem.

I jumped to my feet and sprinted toward the president who was now standing trying to determine what had caused the commotion. Before he recognized that my skin had turned to a faded shade of purple, I leapt on the cement box, maneuvered directly behind him, and gripped his hair.

"Stop him!" Floyd shouted.

It took every bit of strength I had to tear the president's head from his body. The Gore to my left rushed me, but I cleared them out of the way by using the head like a medieval flail.

The president's eyes moved, but the creature had lost the ability to think without its heart. The body stumbled forward a couple of steps before falling to the floor.

I made it to the tunnel after barreling through a line of Gore, but before heading down it, I yelled to Floyd as he reached the last step of the staircase, "Remember, Northampton County Courthouse, 24 hours!"

"Get him!" Floyd shouted! "Save the president!"

I was bulkier entering the tunnel than I was before. My partial Délon transformation had probably added ten to fifteen pounds, and I was at least a couple of inches taller, but I managed to squeeze through the opening and muscle my way through the narrow passageway. I could feel the hands of the Gore grab hold of my heel and pants legs as I pushed my way forward. When the tunnel started to open up, they scurried in front of me. Some of them were carrying various body parts. It appeared their plan was to get far enough in front of me where the tunnel opened up quite a bit more, and reassemble themselves directly in my path.

I picked up my pace and fought to hold onto my anger. It was getting colder and colder, and I felt the Délon in me slipping away. I couldn't let that happen, not yet. I concentrated on everything that pissed me off about my life. I had lost so many friends and family. I had fought so many Destroyers. I had made so many mistakes. It was all so infuriating, but none of it was keeping me angry.

I stopped to catch my breath and slapped the muddy walls of the tunnel. I was going to fail. I was going to let the Gore beat me. And worst of all, I was never going to get Lou back.

I felt the anger come back instantaneously. I was no longer tired. In fact, I had explosive energy. I shot through a row of Gore in the process of assembling themselves and stepped out onto the tracks. I was covered in mud and grime. Turning in the direction I had just come, I saw Floyd making his way towards me.

"Twenty-four hours, Chef Floyd!" With that, I sped down the tracks grasping the president's head by the hair and easily leaving the clumsy Gore behind.

Chapter Twenty-Three

I walked and walked and walked. There was no longer any part of me that was even remotely Délon. The subway tunnels were much draftier and colder than the president's room.

The president's head was much heavier than I had anticipated. It had been no problem when I was operating with a little bit of a rage. But now I was just tired, and my hand cramped as I attempted to keep a tight grip on the president's hair.

There was one major flaw in my plan. I told Floyd to meet me in 24 hours in the Northampton County Courthouse. I had no idea when the 24 hours were up. My only option was to go to the courthouse straight away and wait for him. I didn't even have time to look for the others. I couldn't risk it.

Besides, if I got there before Floyd and the Gore, I might be able to set up a defense system so I could safely make the exchange for the enchanter's head. I had no idea what that defense system would be, but making plans up as I go was kind of my thing now.

I walked until my thighs burned and then plopped down in the middle of one of the track ways. Placing the president's head to my left, I propped my arm on it and fought the urge to nod off. My eyes got heavy and dropped a bit before I forced them open with a jerk. I did this over and over again until the fight to catch some shuteye was just too strong.

"Just a few minutes won't hurt," I mumbled.

Suddenly, I was sitting on the floor of a palace. Ornate furniture and expensive artwork decorated the enormous room. And there was the sound of laughter bouncing off the walls. Dumbfounded, I turned to my left and then to the right. There was no one there. The laughter disappeared, and I yawned.

The laughter came again. Only this time it was followed by the sight of a small boy peeking his head out from behind a large chair.

"Nate?" I said.

He giggled and hid back behind the chair.

Tarek's voice roared, "The boy has a drawing." The large, furry white beast stomped forward from the back of the room with a piece of paper.

I was too groggy to stand, and was startled when I saw Tarek's hand appear in front of me. It was there too quickly. How did he cross the room that fast?

I took the paper from him and unfolded it. It was a rough sketch of a house with four words written across the top, "Maek them a hoam."

"What is this?" I asked.

"It's the final story, Creyshaw."

"It's just a drawing."

"It's the last drawing."

"It doesn't make sense. What does it mean?"

"It means make them a home."

"Make who a home?"

The room exploded outward at the sound of a horn.

I was back on the track with my left arm propped up on the president's head. A pair of headlights was fast approaching.

I hopped up and waved my arms like a madman. The emergency vehicle came to a screeching stop, and Wes threw open the driver's side door. He ran faster than I've ever seen him run. "Oz!"

Still feeling the effects of my escape from the Gore, I bent over and placed my hands on my knees. I barely had any energy left.

Wes placed his hand on my back. "You hurt?"

I shook my head. "Just tired."

"I'm not sure what in the hell that was all about, but don't ever offer yourself up like that again. You hear me?"

I stood up straight with the president's head in my hand. "I won't have to."

"Good Lord, what have you done?" he said stepping away from me.

"I'm just borrowing it."

The president's eyes shifted from me to Wes.

"You want to tell me what for?"

"We exchange this head for the baby-head that's got Lou out of her mind."

A smile slowly formed on his face. "Now that ain't a bad plan."

"I have my moments," I said walking to the truck. "Where's everyone else?"

"A few platforms back. Lou has proven to be a bit of a handful. Takes nearly all of them to watch over her."

"Is she okay?"

He didn't answer.

"Wes, is she okay?"

He scratched his chin and avoided eye contact with me. "She's in sad shape, Oz. Something has got hold of her and is putting her through a crap-load of hurt."

I continued to the truck. "Not for long."

"What's the plan exactly?"

"I need the gorillas and Tyrone. You think you, Vance and Gordy can keep Lou under wraps."

He shook his head. "Don't know about Vance and Gordy, but Minnow should be enough help."

He grabbed my arm and stopped me. "You're plumb wore out. I ain't exactly sure you should be doing nothing but getting some sleep."

"No time."

"There's never time, but I'm telling you to make some."

I looked at the emergency vehicle. "I'll get some sleep while you drive us back to the others."

"That's only about 15 minutes away."

"That'll do."

He groaned and let me go. He knew me well enough to know that arguing with me was pointless. I was going to do what I was going to do. It didn't make a difference what anyone said. Even if they were right, and Wes was right. I was worn out, but I told myself that was a good thing. If I was tired and I knew it, I'd force myself to stay focused, and I'd rely a little more on those around me. I trusted the gorillas and Tyrone with my life, and now I was going to trust them with Lou's life.

As soon as I sat down in the passenger seat of the emergency vehicle, I closed my eyes and fell fast asleep. In fact, I was asleep so quickly it felt like I had just sat down when Wes shook me awake.

"We're here," he said.

I popped an eye open and watched as Tyrone stuck his face in front of mine. "You lose anything to the Gore?"

"Lose anything?"

"You know, a foot or leg or finger?"

I reached down on the floorboard and yanked the president's head up by the hair. "Not only did I not lose anything, I brought something back."

Tyrone's eyes got wide. "What the...?"

Some slime oozed out of the severed head as I climbed out of the emergency vehicle.

"Why do you have that?" Tyrone asked.

"I'll explain later. Get Ajax and Ariabod and load up with as many weapons as you can."

He smiled. "Now you're talking."

I made my way to the platform and set the president's head on it.

"Oz!" Gordy said wrapping me in a bear hug with my back to him. "You came for me! I knew you wouldn't let them pluck me a part."

I let him get the hug out of his system.

When he released me, he spotted the head on the platform and said with a disapproving tone, "What are you doing with that thing?"

"I don't have time to explain, but don't worry, it won't be around long." I pulled myself up on the platform, stood, and immediately took a fist to the face. I stumbled back and managed to keep from hitting the concrete platform surface.

Lou stood over the head of the president with her teeth gritted and hate in her eyes.

"Take it easy," I said. I was torn between wanting to punch her back and giving her a bigger hug than Gordy had given me.

"I should kill you!"

"Wait, wait. I'm not keeping the head."

She squatted down and began stroking the president's hair. "This is a great and noble leader."

"I know you think that, but..."

"I don't just think that," she said. "I know it for a fact. He is full of love and compassion. He let me join his people even though I am useless..."

"You're not useless, Lou. Don't you see? This puke for a leader has convinced you you're useless so you'll feel like you owe him something for taking you in..."

She shook her head and groaned in frustration. "You just don't get it, Oz. The president didn't convince me I'm useless. I am useless..."

"Stop saying that!"

"You stop being so pathetic. Let me go, Oz! Let me be what I'm supposed to be, nothing! I can be nothing with the Gore. At least with them, I have a purpose!"

"You have a purpose with us," I said, feeling more and more like I just wanted to punch her.

"To do what? Hold you back? To keep you from doing what you should be doing? You should be trying to find a way home, Oz!" She saw Wes, Gordy, and Tyrone standing on the tracks below. "You should be trying to find them a way home!"

Wes stepped up. "Little girl, you listen up good. Who was it that found you near the Interstate back there in Manchester all those years ago?"

"You know who," she answered.

"It was me! You wouldn't speak a word back then. And I have to say after hearing you go on about how you ain't real, and we should go on without you, blah, blah, blah... well, you not speaking would be preferable to hearing that crap coming out of your mouth."

She started to cry. "I just don't want to be the reason..."

"Well that's just what you are!" Wes shouted. "You're the reason I didn't lose my mind all those years ago! You're the reason I worked on that stupid old van! You're the reason I got up in the morning, the reason I'd catch myself smiling. You're the reason for just about everything good that's happened to me since the world went to hell in a hand basket." He brushed away a tear. "You, me, Tyrone, Oz, those two hairy apes, and even little smart-ass Gordy, we are family, all of us! It doesn't matter where we come from or how we got here, we are family! And I will not tolerate anything or anyone trying to pull us part. Not even you! You hear me?"

She huffed, "But I serve the Gore..."

"Well, Oz here is working on that. So for now, you just do us all a favor and shut the hell up," Wes said. "No more talk of being useless and not belonging."

I could see in her face that she wanted to continue to make her case, but she didn't. Instead, she picked up the president's head. "Fine, but you're not getting this from me..."

Quick as a flash, Minnow scrambled out of the darkness, ripped the head from her hands and quickly handed it over to me.

"You little..." She growled and lurched forward, but I stepped in front of the little super ninja before she could get to him.

"You can't win this, Lou, so just back off," I said.

She glared at me and then huffed off to the other side of thc platform with the gorillas trailing her.

"You know," Gordy said just as things had gotten quiet. "I'm not really that big of a smart ass."

Chapter Twenty-Four

The courthouse had gotten colder, which meant the temperature outside the building had dropped considerably. Tyrone and I were bundled up as tight as we could as we walked up and down the main hallway. The two gorillas stayed huddled together near the door to the subway system keeping each other warm. At one point, I kicked open a door marked 'Judge's Chambers' at the back of a courtroom and found a judge's robe and heavy coat. Ajax and Ariabod gladly let me cover them up with the two garments.

Tyrone walked out of the courtroom across the hall with another robe and coat. He draped them over the apes and then asked, "How many of those ugly piles of body parts you expecting?"

I pointed to the president's head sitting between Ajax and Ariabod. "We've got their leader... Well part of him anyway, they'll bring as many as they can."

Tyrone chuckled, "I appreciate your confidence in us, Oz, but there's only four of us."

I smiled. "Don't forget there are others."

He raised an eyebrow. "You're actually going to call up the Greasywhoppers."

"Only if I have to. There's still a chance we can make this exchange without it turning into a blood bath."

He shook his head. "You're dreaming."

"Maybe, but if things do go bad, I'll call up our friends. You and the gorillas guard the door to make sure we all have a way out." I pointed to the courtroom on the left. "You and Ajax hide in there. " I whistled to Ariabod. He poked his head out. "And you hide in the courtroom across the hall." The big ape nodded and then covered his head with the robe again.

"What about you?" Tyrone asked. "Where will you be?"

"The other end of the hall. I'll draw as many of them down there as I can."

He looked in the direction I indicated and then said, "You'll be trapped."

"I'll work it out," I said.

"How?"

I shrugged. "I'll know more when I know how many Gore I'm dealing with."

"In other words, you don't know."

"I know enough," I said.

Tyrone waved me off.

"Whatever you do, don't call up the Greasywhoppers. I'm the one that does it. Understand?"

"I won't call them up unless... You know?"

"What?"

"You're dead."

"I'm not going to..." I stopped when I saw the door to the subway slowly push open.

Ariabod and Ajax threw the coats and robes off and spun around ready to pound whatever came through the doorway.

Floyd stepped into the hallway with his hands raised. "I'm alone."

I directed Tyrone to move toward him on the left while I quickly made my way to the right and retrieved the crossbow and arrows propped up against the wall.

"Don't get all jumpy on me," Floyd said. "I'm alone and unarmed."

I loaded the crossbow and aimed it at him. "You appear to be without the enchanter's head, too."

Floyd grinned. "You noticed that, did you?"

"You think I'm playing a game, Floyd?"

"I do. I just don't think you're playing it very well."

I approached with an arrow aimed at a spot between his eyes. "You're wrong if you think I won't kill you."

"Oh, I'm fairly confident you will. It will be the dumbest thing you've ever done, but you'll do it."

"Where is the enchanter's head?"

"In a safe place."

"It better be in a safe place where you can get it quick."

Floyd grinned nervously. "Now you've put me in a tough spot."

I fired the crossbow and grazed his ear with an arrow. He yelped in pain and cupped his hand over the wound. I quickly reloaded. "I'm not interested in making it easy on you."

"You keep shooting arrows at me, and I'm bound to say whatever you want to hear, and that's not going to get us anywhere."

I aimed at his head again.

"The head is not here."

I fired another arrow and grazed the wound I had given him just seconds before. He yelled out in even more pain. "I can do this all day, Floyd!"

"I'm going to give you the head! I promise!"

Reloading the crossbow I asked, "Why should I believe you?"

"Because I am duty bound to serve my president above all other Gore. If I don't, I'll die. If I die, I can't serve the Gore, and all I want to do is serve the Gore." He was trembling, and I had an idea it wasn't from the wound I had given him. He was terrified at the thought he wouldn't be able to serve the Gore.

"Then why didn't you bring the enchanter's head like I told you to?" I asked.

He wiped at the blood that was trailing along his jaw line. "I know your reputation, Oz Griffin."

"My reputation?"

"You are Creyshaw."

"So?"

"So, you are a servant just like me."

I aimed an arrow at his head. "I serve no one."

He grinned. "No, you don't."

"He's talking in circles," Tyrone said. "Just kill him and be done with it."

"You do, and you seal Lou's fate."

I grimaced. "You called me a servant, and then you said I serve no one! What does that mean?"

"You serve the story, Oz. That's what Creyshaw do. I can't trust you to make an honorable deal because if that deal doesn't serve the story, you will violate it."

"So you get the bright idea to show up here unarmed and without what I asked for? How do you think that's going to work out for you?"

"I'm simply changing the story. I'm controlling the exchange."

"How does that make sense?" I asked.

"I'm setting the time and place for this to happen. You'll show up when and where I say. Get it?"

"And you figure that will be safer for you?" I asked.

"I do."

I hesitated and then fired an arrow four feet above his head. "Let's hear it."

"No way, Oz," Tyrone said. "He's setting you up for his own trap."

"We don't have a choice," I said.

"The building with the gold dome in Buffalo."

"Buffalo?" I asked.

"Look for Main Street and Wes Huron."

"Why Buffalo?"

"Because I said Buffalo."

"That's too far away," I said. "We don't have that much time."

He opened the door to the stairwell that lead to the subway. "Head east about ten miles. You'll find a bright blue platform. Go through the door marked Fillmore Line. That will lead you to an express track to Buffalo. There'll be an emergency vehicle waiting for you."

I started for the door.

"Nope," he said. "You give me fifteen minutes before you follow. After that, you get to Buffalo as fast as you can. Look for the gold dome." With that, he disappeared through the doorway.

"I don't trust him," Tyrone said.

"We don't have a choice," I said moving to the open door.

"I still don't like it."

"Neither do I."

Tyrone started to talk, but stopped.

"No use in holding back now," I said. "We've got 15 minutes to kill."

"It's not worth saying."

"Why not?"

"Because it will just piss you off, and you'll end up hating me."

I stared at him. "Then maybe you're right not to say it."

He groaned. "But it's something that has to be said."

"Then say it!"

"Are we doing the right thing?"

I couldn't even imagine what he meant.

"I mean we're going to an awful lot of trouble for..."

"For what?'

"It's just that maybe Lou's right."

"I don't think you should say anymore," I said.

"She's not real, Oz. I mean I know what she's done for us, and I know how you feel about her, but if we do find a way back home, she can't come with us, right? And if we're not looking for a way back home, I don't know what the hell we're doing."

"Stop talking, Tyrone."

"I want to go back, Oz, you know? I just want to go back. Because I was thinking that if I do then maybe Valerie will be there, and I can find her and we can..."

"Valerie is dead, Tyrone! Get over it!"

He skulked towards me. "What did you say?"

"She's dead."

He slowly shook his head. "Don't you say that to me."

"It's true..."

"It's not true! It's only true here, in this twisted, ugly, freak-filled world. In the real world, she's alive!"

"We don't know if that's true. She could be just as dead there as she is here," I said without even having the courage to make eye contact with him.

"Shut up!"

I readied myself for him to come at me with everything he had. Instead, I watched as he fell to his knees and sobbed, repeating the words, "She's alive."

Chapter Twenty-Five

It took two hours to make it to Buffalo. Wes had instructed me to get some sleep on the trip, but I couldn't. There were too many things running through my head, not the least of which was that I was pretty sure my luck was about to run out. I couldn't explain it. I just had a feeling I couldn't win this one.

We reached the surface and faced the coldest temperatures yet. The snow drifted in above us and hid the tops of the skyscrapers stretched out in front of us. Big wet flakes landed gently on the mountains of snow on the streets. The sidewalk we were on remained relatively clear because of the awnings that protected most of the entrances to the buildings. It was icy and slippery, but at least we weren't having to fight our way through the fresh snow that was falling everywhere else.

We came to a cross street and had no choice but to stop because the snow blocked our way. The wind howled and cut through our winter gear. Instinctively, we all huddled around the gorillas and tried to find some warmth.

"We gotta get inside," Wes shouted over the wind. "Ajax and Ariabod are going to freeze to death."

I gripped the handle of the duffle bag that contained the president's head. "Floyd said we have to go to Main

Street and West Huron. We don't have time to stop. We have to keep going."

Wes lifted his head and shielded his eyes with his hands as he looked up and down the sidewalk. "The street signs are covered up. How are we supposed to find Main Street and West Huron? We've got no idea where we are?"

"He said something about a gold dome. 'Look for the gold dome.' That's what he said."

Wes grimaced. "That would be a helpful bit of information if we could see the tops of the buildings. The snow's blocking out everything in the sky and on the road. We gotta be sensible, Oz. We need to get inside one of these buildings and regroup. Warm up."

I shook my head. "No. We're running out of time. I can't risk it. This is Lou's only chance."

Lou was staring down at the ground. She hadn't said two words since her outburst on the platform a few hours ago.

Tyrone broke away from our group. "Gotta pee."

We barely acknowledged him as he moved down the sidewalk and vanished behind a wintery haze.

"Lou won't have no chance at all if we freeze to death," Wes said stomping his feet. "My feet are burning up, and that ain't good. Frostbite is setting in."

"You go inside…"

I stopped when I heard Tyrone shout out. Turning down the sidewalk, we watched as he appeared out of an icy fog.

"What's got into you?" Wes asked.

Tyrone slipped and nearly fell, but righted himself quickly and continued toward us. He was pointing back the way he had come and yelled as he moved in our direction. I finally made out the word, "dome."

I felt my cheeks go flush with excitement. "He found the gold dome," I said.

With me gripping Lou's arm, we broke our huddle and met Tyrone half way. He was breathing heavily when we made it to him. "I saw it. " He said placing his hands on his knees. "I saw the gold dome."

"Where?" I asked.

"At the end of the block. If we hadn't been stopped by the snow bank, we would have walked right past it."

I patted Tyrone on the back. "Yes! You found it!"

Tyrone shot me a dirty look and stepped away from me.

Wes noticed the exchange. "What's got into you two? Tyrone's been pouting ever since you got back from the courthouse."

"It's not important," I said. "We need to get moving..."

"Hold on," Wes said. "What's the plan?"

Tyrone shook his head in disgust. "Oz isn't big on plans."

Vance threw up his arms. "Then me and Minnow are out. I'm not walking that boy in there without some kind of strategy."

"Then don't go," I shouted. "You're useless anyway."

Wes yanked me aside not noticing that I had hold of Lou. He pulled both of us away from everyone else. "We're about to step into a mess, and you ain't doing nothing but whittling down our forces..."

"He can barely move..." I started to say.

"Maybe, but he and the boy are a package deal. And he's right, we need a plan."

"There's no plan to be had, Wes. This is Floyd's move."

"Floyd's move? Son, did your brain just drop out of your head?"

"He never had much of a brain," Lou said with a wicked grin. "He's going to get you all killed."

"Shut up, little girl," Wes said.

"Wes," I said, "we have to face the facts. Floyd is calling the shots here."

"That may well be, but let's at least formulate some kind of plan."

I sighed in frustration. "I'm listening."

Wes nodded. "That's more like it." Stepping back, he mumbled something about a good plan and just kept mumbling.

"I'm not hearing a plan, Wes."

"Well, there's only one thing we can do."

"And that is?"

"Get rid of our liabilities before we go into battle."

I smiled. "I agree. We should send Vance away..."

"He's not a liability," Wes said.

"Then who?" I asked.

"I told you before you are plumb wore out. You ain't thinking straight, and you are bound to make a mistake that will cost us plenty if you're involved with what needs to get done in that dome." He motioned to Ariabod. "Grab hold of him."

Ariabod lurched forward and wrapped his massive hand around my wrist.

"What are you doing?" I said in a panic trying to pull away.

"I'm doing what I should've done a long time ago. I'm taking charge." He ripped the duffle bag out of my hand.

"I have to make the exchange! Let me go!" I pulled and pulled, but it was no use. "What happened to not whittling down our forces?"

Ignoring me Wes said to Ariabod, "Take him and Lou into that building behind you,"

"Wes, what are you doing?" Tyrone asked.

"This is for the best, son."

"But… I mean it's Oz… he's the leader."

"Which is why I can't let him walk into what's sure to be a trap. He's thinking with his heart and a brain that's half asleep."

"Stop him, Tyrone," I said. "He's making a huge mistake. We'll never get Lou back."

"I'll get her back," Wes said. "You're going to have to trust me this time." He started to move down the sidewalk.

"Don't let him do this, Tyrone! I know you're mad at me, but you know this isn't right."

Tyrone took a step toward Wes, but Ajax let out a garbled growl. It was clear Wes and the gorillas had worked something out behind my back.

"We'll make the exchange without you, boy," Wes said.

"And what am I supposed to do?" I asked, spitting bile and venom.

"You'll wait with Ariabod and Lou and like it." Wes said with a smile.

I made another attempt to break free from Ariabod, but it was no use. He dragged Lou and me to the door of the building behind us and easily pushed it open, breaking a deadbolt in the process.

The huge gorilla pulled us to a leather sofa and sat us down. The place was in bad shape, but it was still obvious that it was once a fancy hotel.

Ariabod still had hold of my wrist. I twisted and jerked, but it was impossible to break free.

"You're hurting me, you dumb ape."

"And what do you think you're doing to me?" Lou asked.

Ariabod snorted and snarled.

"You can let me go. I won't run," I said.

Ariabod almost appeared to roll his eyes.

"Same goes for me," Lou said. "I couldn't run if I wanted to. I can barely walk on my own thanks to you."

"You're breaking my wrist," I said ignoring Lou.

I felt him ease up just the slightest in his grip.

"Better," I said.

He seemed to relax.

I studied his leathery face and changed tactics. "We should be helping them, you know. We're warriors, that's what we do. We shouldn't be here, and you know it."

He ignored me.

"What if they get killed? What then? How are you going to feel about yourself?"

He huffed.

I sat back in frustration and tapped my foot on the dust covered floor.

He barked and jerked my arm, signaling that I was annoying him.

I tapped faster.

"Stop it," Lou said.

Ariabod snarled and tugged me to the hard marble floor of the hotel lobby, breaking the grasp I had on Lou's arm. She attempted to stand, but quickly dropped back down to the sofa. She hadn't been exaggerating when she said she couldn't run.

"Easy, big guy. You trying to pull my arm out of its socket?" I worked to get up on my knees. "Okay, if I can't guilt you into doing the right thing, then let's at least find the kitchen in this place and see if there's anything we can eat."

He tried to pretend like he was uninterested in my request, but I could tell he was thinking it over.

"C'mon. I bet they got all kinds of canned goods."

He did a half turn in my direction.

"Peas, corn, peaches…"

He woofed at the thought of canned peaches. He started to drag me to the back of the room.

"Hold up."

He stopped and gave me the evil eye for delaying his hunt for peaches.

"This will go a lot faster if you let me go."

He huffed.

"I won't run."

His shifted from me to the back of the room.

"I'll get in front of you with Lou. There's no way I can get around you and make it to the door without you catching me."

He sighed and slowly released my arm.

I rubbed my wrist and helped Lou to her feet. She didn't have the energy to fight me.

Ariabod shoved me in front of him.

"Okay, okay, I'm going."

We stepped over the clutter and debris in the lobby and made our way down a hallway that a sign said led to a restaurant. The hotel had been ransacked a dozen times over, and I was pretty sure we wouldn't find a single crumb of food. I was just biding my time. I had to get to the building with the gold dome. If Ariabod wasn't going to do the right thing, I needed to find a way to put some distance between him and me. What to do with Lou was another problem.

I scanned every inch of the restaurant as we walked through searching for my best escape route. Tables, chairs, and broken glass littered a good bit of the floor. I could make a run for it and hope the debris would slow Ariabod down. But knowing the big ape, he'd catch me before I found my way out and drag Lou and me through the shards of glass to teach me a lesson.

I pushed the kitchen door open and stepped inside with Lou so Ariabod could enter. The room was large, but jammed with equipment and filled with plenty of counter space. Unlike the dining room, it was neat and tidy. It didn't make sense. It should have been turned upside down by survivors scouring for food. Instead, it looked like it probably did just before operating hours back when the hotel was full of hungry guests.

The pristine appearance of the kitchen made Ariabod nervous, too. The hair on his back and shoulders was on end. He knuckle-walked forward, sniffing the air as he did.

"Something's not right," I said.

He kept moving forward, having completely forgotten about me.

It dawned on me that this was my chance. To my right was a rack of pots and pans. I could grab a hold of it and yank it down. If I left Lou behind, Ariabod would hesitate. I was positive he wouldn't want to leave her behind.

Ariabod stopped. A second or two passed before he let out a soft hoot. I was now a distant concern in his mind.

I put my hand on the rack and tightened my grip until my knuckles turned white.

Ariabod pounded his chest.

I eased up on my grip. Someone or something was in the kitchen, that was pretty clear. If I pulled down the rack and took off, I'd be leaving Ariabod to fend for himself. I'd be abandoning him just like he abandoned the others. I hesitated and then re-tightened my grip. The others needed me more.

My muscles tightened in my shoulder, and I told myself I'd count to three in my head and pull the rack down. I barely got to two when I felt something poking me in my side.

"Don't you dare do it," I heard a young child's voice say.

I turned slowly and saw the pale blue eyes of a young girl staring back at me. She was holding a large carving knife to my side.

Ariabod wheeled around and huffed menacingly.

The girl pressed slightly harder on the knife which made me yelp in pain. "Hold your furry friend back," she said.

"Who are you?" I asked.

"I own this hotel."

Ariabod pounded his fists on the floor.

"Tell him to back off!" She pressed the knife into me harder, and it felt like the tip broke the skin.

"Okay, okay, okay," I said waving to Ariabod, hoping he would listen to me for once. Amazingly he did.

She seemed to relax. "Now, why are you three in my hotel?"

"We were just getting in out of the cold."

With the knife still touching me, she leaned against the swinging door to look into the dining room. "Are you alone?"

"No," I said. "Well, we are, but we shouldn't be." I furrowed my brow at Ariabod.

"What's that supposed to mean?"

"It means we have to leave, and help some friends."

She shook her head. "Nope. I can't let that happen."

I looked at her and smiled. "Excuse me?"

"I can't let you leave. I don't know you. You might be with them. I let you go, and you'll lead them right back to me."

"Okay," I said, "I don't know who this 'them' is, and I don't really care. We are leaving."

"I'll ram this knife in your gut if you even so much as flinch."

"And Ariabod will snap your neck before I start bleeding."

She groaned.

"We're strangers. That's all we are. We don't want any trouble."

"Then why did you come to my hotel?"

"We were just looking for shelter. There's a blizzard outside."

She almost laughed. "You must be strangers because there's been a blizzard for nearly a year now."

"A year?"

She hesitated. “Maybe longer. Keeping time isn’t an easy thing in a world with no clocks.”

Lou’s eyes started to flutter, and she took a clumsy step back.

“Stop that,” thc girl said.

Lou lazily held out a hand and took another step back.

“Tell her to stop,” the girl said.

“Are you okay, Lou?” I asked.

She didn’t answer. Her eyes started to roll back in her head.

“Lou?”

She fell back, but Ariabod caught her before she hit the floor.

“She’s out,” the girl said.

“Let me go,” I said. “I need to help her.”

The girl hesitated and then pulled the knife away.

I raced to Lou’s side and placed my hand on her forehead. “She’s ice cold.”

“Probably dead,” the girl said.

I took my coat off and with Ariabod’s help, we wrapped it around her shoulder. “She’s breathing.”

The girl stood over me and then exited the kitchen. Before Ariabod and I could exchange confused looks, she was back with a stack of blankets. “Put your coat back on before you freeze to death. You can cover her up with these.”

I did as she suggested and watched in horror as Lou started to twitch uncontrollably.

“What’s going on with her?” the girl asked.

I stood up. “Something must be wrong.”

“Well, duh. She’s popping about like a piece of bacon on a skillet.”

"No," I said. "I mean something must be wrong at the gold dome."

The girl's expression turned to horror. "What do you know about the gold dome?"

"I have some friends who went inside."

Her eyes opened wide. "You mean you HAD some friends that went inside."

"What does that mean?" I asked.

"It means the gold dome isn't a place that people come of out alive."

I turned to Ariabod. "You see? We should have gone with them!"

"Why would you want to do a stupid thing like that?" the girl asked. "That is Dr. Bashir's sanctuary."

The name rattled around in my ears and created a ringing sound. The tone of it nearly made me dizzy. "Dr. Bashir?"

She shook her head. "He's a bad man. A bad, bad man."

"I know he is," I said. My mind felt like it was going to explode. My eyes shifted from side to side as I tried to catch hold of a single idea, one brilliant concept that would make us all safe.

The girl spoke in a panic. "Does Dr. Bashir know you're here?"

I didn't answer.

She grabbed my arm and shook. "Does he know you're in my hotel?"

I slowly shook my head and stood. "No, but I've got a feeling he's waiting for me in the gold dome."

Ariabod was apprehensive. He had been ordered to keep me away from the dome, but he sensed something was wrong, too.

"You can't come," I said to him.

He growled.

"I know it's not in your nature to listen to me, but we don't have a whole lot of time here. Someone has got to watch over Lou. If Bashir is in the gold dome, he's waiting for me, not you."

He huffed and then sat on his haunches.

"No, no, no," the girl said. "You're not going over there. He'll find out I'm here. I can't let you go."

I rolled my eyes. "I may have given you the wrong impression before when I let you sneak up on me and stick a knife in my side. I will hurt you if you try to stand in my way."

She placed herself in front of the door holding onto her knife. She gripped and re-gripped it over and over again, and her expression told me she was not that skilled at using it.

I took a single step in her direction, and she flinched, dropping the knife in the process. I smiled. "It'll be okay. Ariabod will look out for you."

I exited the kitchen and headed to the meet the man who'd ended my world.

Chapter Twenty-Six

There was nothing to do, but enter the building. It was useless to try and come up with a plan or sneak in or even burst in like a madman. This was all about to be over for me. I knew that. I had no weapons. It was too cold for me to tap into the Délon in me. I couldn't even bring myself to hope that I'd survive. All I wanted is for my friends to be alive.

I stood just inside the door and peered up at the domed ceiling. It took several seconds of looking through the dust and dirt before I realized that there was a painting on it. I saw the image of a scorpion and a goat before my attention was diverted by the sound of somebody moaning.

I turned to my right and saw Tyrone on the floor. He was covered in blood. I stepped toward him, but he waved me off. "I'll live." He pushed himself to a seated position. "Should have had a plan, Oz. Should have had a plan."

"Where are the others?"

He pointed to a sculpture of a large brass bowl in the middle of the room. "That way."

"I'm going to get you all out of here," I said, having no idea if that was even remotely possible.

He coughed and then groaned in pain before saying, “Not all of us.”

I hesitated while I quickly mulled over what he’d said. I didn’t want to believe what Tyrone was telling me. I couldn’t get them all out because someone was already dead. As I moved forward, I found myself dreading what I was about to see. I even stopped at one point and considered running back out into the snow, back to the entrance to the subway, back through the tunnels, back to a place where I would never know who was dead.

Gordy was on the other side of the sculpture. He was leaning against the base with his forehead resting on his knees and his arms wrapped around his shins. He was weeping. On the floor next to him was Ajax, on his back, motionless. I couldn’t force myself to look at him because I knew if I did I wouldn’t see him breathing. I told myself as long as I didn’t know for sure, he was alive. He was alive.

When I heard a familiar hoot-grunt, I sighed. It wasn’t just wishful thinking on my part. He really was alive.

Approaching him, I saw that he was bloody, but he was breathing steadily.

I knelt down between Gordy and Ajax.

Gordy barked out a scream when I touched his shoulder.

“Relax,” I said. “It’s just me.”

He held up a finger to his lips and silently shushed me. Pointing behind me, he whispered, “They’re still here.”

I looked in the direction he was pointing but only saw a long, high counter. I was about to tell him that I didn't see anything when I spotted Minnow standing on the other side of the room with his knife in hand.

With a mixture of fear and anger, I asked Gordy the question I wasn't sure I wanted to know the answer to. "Where's Wes?"

He buried his head and cried even harder.

I shook him. "Tell me where Wes is."

He couldn't answer.

"Gordy…"

A man's voice boomed through the domed structure. "I have waited for this moment for so, so long!"

I stood, but couldn't see the source of the voice.

"You have ruined so much for me you stupid, meddling boy!"

"Show yourself," I said.

A tall figure appeared in a dark doorway behind the long counter.

"Bashir?"

He clucked out a laugh and stepped through the doorway. He was a thin, bearded man with a heavily scarred face and long, almost bushy hair. "Why doesn't it surprise me that you know who I am?"

"Where's Wes?"

"You broke the rules!"

"Tell me where Wes is!"

"Stevie broke the rules!"

"I don't care who broke your stupid rules! Where is Wes?"

Bashir moved around the counter, and I saw for the first time that he was carrying the enchanter's head. Holding it up he said, "Floyd gave it to me."

I instantly thought of a million ways I could end Floyd's life.

"You were not supposed to beat the Takers."

Before the echo of the sentence died down, I heard the chatter of the Takers as they made their way out of their universe and began to gather in a slobbering hoard behind Bashir.

"Stevie did not tell the story as I had instructed him to. You were supposed to die. You were his tormentor. You bullied him. He should have gladly written it with you becoming nothing but a rotting corpse at the end. He should have delighted in writing it that way."

"You want me dead? Then kill me. Just let my friends go, and I'll let you do whatever you want to me."

"Are you trying to make a bargain with me? With what? You have nothing to bargain with."

I fell to my knees and clasped my hands together. "I'm begging you to let my friends go."

"I'm not going anywhere."

I turned to my right and saw Tyrone hunched over, holding his ribs with his left arm, and holding onto his knife with his other hand.

To my left, Gordy stood shaking like a leaf with a loaded crossbow. "Me either."

Ajax rolled over and used every bit of strength he had to stand on all fours.

Minnow pounded his chest and held his fist in the air.

Bashir shook his head in disgust. "I don't understand this thing in you that propels people to believe in you, Oz."

Floyd appeared from behind the counter. "The famous Oz Griffin is on his knees."

I responded by glaring at him.

"I have to tell you I have been so unimpressed with you."

"You served your purpose, Floyd," Dr. Bashir said. "Take your silly president's head and go back to your Gore."

Floyd disappeared for a second behind the counter and then reappeared holding the duffle bag containing the president's head. "We have some unfinished business, Dr. Bashir."

"You set this up?" I asked Floyd.

He climbed on the counter. "Not me, no. I was prepared to make the exchange with you back at the courthouse, but the good doctor came to me and offered me a deal that I couldn't refuse. I give him the enchanter's head and then convince you that our little trade has to take place here."

"Why here?" I asked.

"Ask the doc," Floyd said.

Bashir smirked. "I have my reasons."

I stood. "What else?"

"What else what?" Floyd asked.

"What else are you getting for your part? You were going to get the president's head anyway. There has to be something else you're getting for bringing us here."

He jumped off the counter and grabbed the duffle bag. "I am indeed. I'm getting what I've always wanted since I first laid eyes on a pile of body parts back in Charleston in the aquarium. I'm joining the Gore."

"But you can't," I said. "You're not real. The Gore won't take you."

"A problem that Dr. Bashir has offered to fix."

"How?"

"By making me real."

I raised an eyebrow and looked at Dr. Bashir. His evil grin told me everything I needed to know. Turning back to Floyd, I let a smile slowly float across my face.

"What are you smiling at?" Floyd asked.

"He's lying."

"Who's lying?"

I pointed at Dr. Bashir. "He can't make you real. He lied to you."

Floyd's face drained of all color. "That's not true. He said it. He said that if I gave him the enchanter's head and brought you here, he'd make me real. That was our deal. Tell him, Dr. Bashir."

Bashir cleared his throat. "As I said, Floyd, you're services are no longer required. You may go."

Floyd approached him. "But you said you'd make me real. Make me real. Do what you said you'd do."

Bashir rolled his eyes. "I have far more pressing matters to attend to. I'll fulfill our bargain when I have resolved this issue."

"No, do it now. We made a deal."

"I'm losing my patience, Floyd. Leave now!"

Floyd didn't listen. "We made a deal!"

While Bashir was distracted, I turned to Tyrone and whispered. "Where's Wes?"

He simply responded by shaking his head and pointing to the long counter.

"Is he alive?"

Tyrone shrugged. "Things got out of hand. I lost track of everybody. I just heard... him screaming."

I focused my attention on the counter, but was quickly distracted when Dr. Bashir roared in frustration and anger.

"If you insist on prattling on, my dear Floyd, you will learn what kind of power I can wield!" Dr. Bashir snapped his fingers and a Taker advanced on the Gore's servant.

Floyd backed away. "I have friends, too." He whistled, and a horde of Gore poured into the dome through the front door.

Sounding amused Dr. Bashir said, "Your friends are nothing more than the grotesquely cobbled ruins of a world that no longer exists. They have no place or power here. This is my domain."

"Maybe," Floyd said still backing away from the slowly advancing Taker. "But you have something they really, really want."

He held up the enchanter's head. "I'm afraid I still have a use for this vile artifact..."

"That's not what I was talking about," Floyd said.

"What then?" He asked, watching as Floyd continued to retreat.

"Hands!"

The Gore began their chanting.

The Takers responded by chattering to each other.

A fight was about to erupt, and we would be caught in the middle. If I had the enchanter's head, I would welcome the chaos of a battle between the Gore and the Takers, but without the head, there was a huge risk of losing any chance of getting my hands on it.

I stood and stepped forward. "I'm starting to feel left out. This whole thing was put together for me, but you two act like I'm not even here. Normally, I wouldn't mind, but I need the enchanter's head."

Bashir smiled. "Ah, yes, the enchanter's head." Holding it by the thin, fine hair, he shook it violently.

I knew then that was what was causing Lou to shake earlier.

I slowly moved forward. "How do we make this happen?"

"Happen?" Bashir asked.

"What do I have to do to get that head?"

Bashir smiled and said simply, "Surrender."

Without hesitating, I said, "Then I surrender."

He furrowed his brow. "That's it?"

"That's it." I motioned for Tyrone to join me.

"Where's the hero Oz? The Oz that never gives up? The Oz that always thinks there's a way out?"

"This is my way out. You set the enchanter's head on the floor, and let Tyrone and the others leave with it, and I surrender. I won't fight you. You have my word."

"His word?" Floyd said with a snicker. He was now kneeling over the duffle bag at the other end of the room. The Taker hovered just a few feet away from him, snarling and ready to attack. "His word means nothing." He unzipped the bag, and a gaggle of hands quickly converged on its contents. In a matter of seconds, they retrieved the president's head and reattached it to its Gore body.

"My servant is correct about that," the president said stretching his neck. "Leader Oz does not honor the deals he makes." He moved around the sculpture in the center of the room. "He is not to be trusted."

Bashir smiled. "They have a point, Oz."

I nodded. "I know I lied to you, Mr. President, but I had to. Lou was going to die."

"This is for the useless girl?"

"She's not useless. You are nothing without your head and heart. My people are nothing without Lou."

The president considered my explanation.

"Besides it doesn't matter now because things have changed," I said.

"How so?" Bashir asked.

I shrugged. "I can't go home."

Bashir raised an eyebrow. "You expect me to believe you've given up hope..."

"It's not about hope. I just know how this story has been written. Lou is what she is. I can't change that. I don't want to change that. She wouldn't be Lou if I did. And, I know that means she can't go back with me. So that means I won't go back because I wouldn't be me without her."

Bashir hesitated and then said sarcastically, "Isn't that just so sweet?"

The president stepped forward. "You are connected to the girl?"

I nodded. "I am."

"Like the Gore, you share parts from the same donor?"

I grinned and said, "In a way, yes."

"And the others in your group, are you connected to them as well?"

"I am."

After considering this new information, the president turned to Bashir. "You are to give leader Oz the enchanter's head so he can release the girl from service. Our deal is no longer valid."

Bashir laughed. "I'm so happy you were touched by the boy's love story, but I'm afraid it didn't work on me. Oz isn't capable of loving anything."

"I believe his feelings to be genuine," the president said.

"That's wonderful for you! But I know him too well. This love-struck putrid warrior is a monster. He tortured a boy for years because the boy wasn't perfect. Because he wasn't like everyone else. Your leader Oz reminded this boy just how different he was every opportunity he had. Someone so despicable isn't capable of thinking of anyone but himself. He cares nothing for Lou or any of these other wretched souls that travel with him. He cares only for himself."

"You're wrong!" Gordy said. "Oz is a good person. He's put his own life on the line dozens of times for all of us..."

"Because he had no choice," Bashir said. "Stevie wrote him that way."

Gordy was still shaking, but he moved in front of me. "Did you ever think that Stevie wrote him that way because that's the way Oz really is inside?"

"Gordy," I said, "it doesn't matter."

He turned to me. "It does matter, Oz. I was there with you when you picked on Stevie. We all did it. You weren't even the worst one. If anything, I was. We basically forced you to bully Stevie."

I shook my head. "I still bullied him. It doesn't really matter why..."

"But don't you get it?" Gordy said. "It does matter. This is what Stevie wants you to see."

"What are you talking about?"

"You think you were this crappy kid that did horrible things. You still think you're bad, but now you're doing good things to make up for what you are. You're not bad. You never were. You're good. You always have been good. You just did some bad things. Stevie understood that. He wants you to understand it."

I didn't reply. I just tried to absorb what he had said and decide if it mattered.

He shrugged and said, "Of course, I was a total piece of crap, but that's not important right now."

Out of the corner of my eye, I saw Minnow make a move towards Dr. Bashir. I pushed Gordy aside and tried to stop him, but before I could even take two steps, Minnow was standing next to Ajax with the enchanter's head in his hands, and Bashir was nursing a cut on his arm.

Bashir was about to direct the Takers to attack, but I held up my hands. "Stop!"

For whatever reason, Bashir held the slobbering Greasywhoppers back.

"This changes nothing," I said. "I still surrender. Just let my friends leave."

Bashir chuckled. "I still find it odd that you think you have any leverage with which to negotiate."

The president stood tall. "We are in alliance with leader Oz."

"Mr. President," Floyd said. "We can't do that."

The president was clearly unhappy with his servant. "Are you questioning my decision, Chef Floyd?"

"No," Floyd said. "I just feel it's my duty to remind my president that Oz travels with the boy, the killer of Gore."

The president hesitated and then said, "Circumstances have changed. The boy is forgiven his crimes against the Gore."

"But, you can't do that! He has to pay..."

"Servant!" The president's booming voice filled every inch of the dome. "I have given the directive! I will not tolerate any more questions on the matter! We are in alliance with leader Oz and all he is connected to!"

"And that threat is just as laughable as it was before," Dr. Bashir said.

The president ordered the Gore to move aside. They did so quickly, and an enchanter stepped forward from the back of the room with a single severed hand covering its mouth. The enchanter approached the Taker that had forced Floyd to retreat. The fingers of the severed hand spread apart and allowed a single whispered sound to escape and reach the ear of the Greasywhopper.

The Taker turned from a seething monster to subservient beast. It stepped in line with the Gore and joined in the low chant.

Gordy's shaking became less pronounced. "Well, that's a neat trick."

The president returned his attention to Bashir. "I don't wish to turn anymore because they are useless creatures. We cannot use any of their parts, but I will do so if you direct them to attack."

Bashir's face twisted into a scowl.

"This isn't a hard choice," I said to Bashir. "I've already told you I surrender. All you have to do is let the others leave."

Bashir breathed deeply. "Very well. They may go."

"No," Tyrone said. "I'm not leaving..."

"You are," I said. "I'm the key. I finally know what that means. I'm the key to everything we've been through. I'm the reason you're in danger. If I go with Dr. Bashir, you'll be safe." I turned to Bashir. "That's right, isn't it? No harm will come to them if I surrender?"

He groaned. "They are nothing to me. You are the one that broke the rules."

I repeated, "And no harm will come to them if I surrender?"

"I can only promise that if they continue north they will not be pursued by Destroyers. The creatures formed by the chaos of this world are beyond my influence. But that chaos would not exist if not for you. So it is likely to subside once you are in my care."

"Get everyone to the tunnels and head north," I said to Tyrone. "There have to be more underground warehouses stocked with supplies. Those are your new homes. You're in charge now."

He looked at me trembling, eyes bloodshot, his teeth bared. "I don't want to be in charge."

I nodded. "I know how you feel. I never did either."

"The longer you make me wait," Dr. Bashir said, "the less interest I have in keeping our deal."

"There are two others," I said. "They're part of the deal, too."

He shrugged. "Very well."

I ran to the counter and climbed on top of it. Wes was lying in a pool of blood on the floor. I jumped down and squatted next to him. "Wes?"

He didn't answer.

"Wes?"

"He's not going to answer," Vance said.

He sat propped against the wall. His rifle butt leg was missing, and his face was swollen from the beating he had taken.

"He tried to help me. One of your Greasywhoppers broke off my peg leg. Was about to eat me up. Wes jumped it from behind and nearly got the best of it before two more of them yanked him to the ground and started ripping him to shreds with those awful claws." He took the glasses off his face. "Saw the whole damn thing because of these stupid glasses. Wish like hell Wes had never given them to me."

A soft wheeze of a breath escaped Wes' mouth.

"He's alive," I said in a daze. "Wes, can you hear me?"

His eyes opened, and he let out another noisy breath.

"Wes, we're going to get you out of here."

Blood dripped off his brow and into his eye, but he didn't notice.

I stood and was surprised to see the president standing just on the other side of the counter. "Leader Oz, you are concerned for your constituent?"

I shook my head. "He's not my constituent. He's my friend."

The Gore leader peered over the counter. "Perhaps he should join the Gore. I could arrange for his head and heart to remain as a unit."

"No!" I blurted. "No, that's nice of you to offer, but my other friends need him."

The president sniffed. "I fear he will not live much longer."

"He'll live," I said.

The president motioned for the Taker that was under the influence of the enchanter to join him. "Then let us put our newest servant to work." To the Taker he said, "You are to carry this injured friend wherever Oz directs."

I looked at the Greasywhopper and considered turning the president down, but there was no way Tyrone and Gordy could carry Wes. Ajax was even too weak to do it. I eventually nodded and said, "To the hotel to the left and across the street."

The Taker effortlessly climbed over the counter and scooped Wes up in its massive arms. Before it could carry him off, I stopped it.

I leaned in and whispered to Wes, "Everyone will be safe now. You can stop worrying." I moved away and watched as the Taker carried Wes around the corner and towards the door.

Gordy approached. "He's not going to be happy. Neither is Lou. Hell, I'm not happy about this."

I shrugged and smiled. "It's Tyrone's job to put up with you jerks now, not mine."

He scanned the group of Takers and then turned back to me. "Isn't it our thing to fight for each other? I mean I'm not that great at it, but... It's you, Oz. We're just supposed to leave you behind?"

"Don't think of it as leaving me behind. Think of it as our new way of fighting for each other."

He raised an eyebrow and said, "That may be the stupidest thing ever to come out of your mouth."

Vance groaned.

I motioned in his direction. "You think you can give Vance a hand."

Gordy rolled his eyes. "Oh man, I always have to do the extra work."

I watched as Vance put his arm around Gordy's shoulder, and they both struggled to stand on the three legs between them.

I saw someone approach out of the corner of my eye. Startled, I whirled around and instinctively took a step back. Ajax, still a bit woozy, sat on his haunches and stared at me for a few seconds before he went through a series of signs.

"Sorry, big guy, I don't know what you're saying."

The gorilla continued to sign.

"Ajax, buddy..."

With his arm draped around Gordy's shoulder, Vance said, "He says he's proud to call you his brother."

"I thought you didn't know sign language," I said

"I don't need to know sign language to know what he's saying."

Ajax stood and approached me walking on two legs. I didn't recall ever seeing him doing that before. Before I could react, he wrapped me in a gentle hug. Afterwards, he huffed and walked on all fours towards Tyrone.

Tyrone choked back tears and said, "Don't make us do this, Oz."

I ignored him. "You'll find Ariabod and Lou in the kitchen of the hotel. Don't burn the enchanter's head until you can get down into the tunnels and get a few platforms north of here."

He nodded.

"Tell Lou... tell her I'm dead."

"Dead?"

"And one more thing. Make them a home."

He looked at me confused. "What does that mean?"

"I don't know," I said. "But I've got a feeling if you figure it out, you'll see Valerie again."

I watched as the warriors that had helped me survive the end of the world headed for the door. The Gore stepped aside to give them a clear path. Minnow exited first, followed by Ajax and then Gordy and Vance.

Tyrone stopped at the open doorway, raised his fist in the air and shouted, “I am Creyshaw!”

Chapter Twenty-Seven

When the last Gore left the building, I was left facing Dr. Bashir and his army of slobbering Greasywhoppers. They snarled and snapped their massive jaws while Bashir moved to the sculpture. He snapped his fingers. Two Takers stepped out of the ranks, ran to the back office and reappeared with two chairs. They placed them near the sculpture.

Bashir took several seconds to arrange the chairs just as he wanted them. It wasn't enough that they were facing each other. They had to be in perfect alignment with one another. When I sat, my chair scooted to the left ever so slightly. He readjusted his chair's position to be the mirror image of mine.

"I'm glad we're alone," he said.

"You mean besides all those monsters over there," I said motioning toward the Takers with my head.

"Do they make you nervous?"

"Let's just say we're not exactly friends. As long as they're around, you can't expect me to be totally relaxed."

He laughed and snapped his fingers. "They're no longer needed." The Takers vanished without a trace.

I smiled and said, "You're going to have to teach me that trick."

He leaned in and stared at me. "Stevie used to go on and on about something being inside you, some sort of magic or some such nonsense. I thought I had broken him of the notion. I was sure of it." He leaned back. "I certainly don't see it."

I didn't respond.

"Shall I tell you what I do see?"

"I've got a feeling you're going to tell me whether I want to know or not."

He grinned. "You are perceptive. I'll give you that much. I see darkness in you, Oz, a horrible, destructive darkness."

I laughed.

"I fail to see the humor."

"You forced the kids in your care to destroy the world, and you call me destructive?"

"I showed them a path to justice for the way they were treated. The justice they found was equal in measure to the hell you and the others like you forced them to live."

I shook my head. "You filled their heads with hate, but only because you couldn't fill their hearts with hate. Yeah, we treated them like crap, and yeah, we should have to pay for that, but they didn't want to do it, not the way you taught them. I couldn't figure out why the Storytellers created Creyshaw, but coming here, finally meeting you, I get it now."

"Enlighten me."

"Because we are the only ones that have what it takes to beat you. You put them through a far worse hell than any of us did."

"I taught them to stand up for themselves..."

"No, you tried to teach to them how to be bullies like us. All they ever wanted was to be accepted for who they were, but you wanted them to destroy the people that didn't accept them. They knew that was wrong..."

"They knew nothing!"

I settled back. "Careful, doctor. That almost sounded insensitive."

He quickly leaned forward and shoved his finger in my face. "Don't get smug with me, Oz. I helped the boy you discarded like trash."

"By terrifying him? By making him feel like the only way to end his misery was to wipe out everything, including himself?"

"His suicide is on you, not me!"

"You still don't get it! Stevie didn't kill himself because of what I did to him. He killed himself because he wanted everyone to finally see what you really are, what you really do to the kids you treat! We're here to stop you!"

He laughed.

I caught my breath and said, "Now I'm the one who fails to see the humor."

"Look around you, Oz. There is no 'we' here to stop me. It's just you."

I smiled. "Maybe you should look again."

Before he could react, a large gorilla hand appeared behind him and yanked him to the floor. The doctor managed to get out the beginnings of a scream when a piece of duct tape was quickly placed over his mouth.

Gordy stood with a grin, "No calling out the Greasywhoppers, doc."

Tyrone, still protecting his sore ribs with one arm, appeared next to Ariabod. "How do you like that? I've been leader for twenty minutes, and I already saved your ass."

I sighed with relief. "I was starting to think for the first time in your life you were going to listen to me and actually leave me behind."

"I gotta admit that was a pretty good show you put on with all those hokey goodbyes and crap," Gordy said.

"I had to convince the good doctor that I meant it, didn't I?"

"The only problem is you almost convinced us, too," Tyrone said. "What were you going to do, if we really left you behind?"

I shrugged. "I was kind of making it up as I went along. So what made you come back?" I asked.

"It was my idea," Gordy said. "Once we had the enchanter's head in a safe place, I convinced Tyrone we should go back with Ariabod and save you..."

Tyrone cleared his throat and rolled his eyes. "It was those stupid sticks I couldn't break. We need our brain."

I smiled. "You mean I actually got through to you?"

"Don't get used to it."

"Sticks?" Gordy said. "Coming back was so totally my idea… most of it... part of it… I'm the one that said we should bring the duct tape."

I patted him on the shoulder. "Nicely done, Gordy. Nicely done."

"So, what do we do with him?" Gordy asked, standing over Dr. Bashir.

I stared at the doctor as he struggled against Ariabod's grip.

"Tape his hands together."

Tyrone looked disappointed. "Shouldn't we just... you know... kill him."

I shook my head. "He's got more value as a prisoner than he does as a corpse."

I watched as they flipped Bashir over. Tyrone held the doctor's hands behind his back while Gordy thoroughly bound them with tape. When he was satisfied there was no way our new prisoner could free his hands, we all helped Bashir to his feet.

"Got any idea what do to do with him?" Tyrone asked.

I looked around the dome and then said, "He brought us to the place for a reason, which is why we should get out of here as fast as we can."

"Plenty of empty rooms in the hotel," Gordy said.

Tyrone added, "And Wes needs some time to heal before we go anywhere."

I nodded. "Then the hotel will be our home for awhile."

We headed for the door.

"Then what?" Tyrone asked.

"First, we make sure the building is secure..."

"No," Tyrone said. "That's not what I meant. Where do we go from here? Are we going home or not?"

I thought about his question before nodding. "We are, but we're going to make them a home first."

"And who is 'them'?" Gordy asked.

"I don't know," I said and then threw in, "yet."

We stopped in our tracks when we heard the door to the building opening. I lost all sense of my surroundings when I saw Lou rush in from the cold. She stood in the open doorway ready for a fight. She was coming to save me because that's what we did, she and I. We saved each other.

I wasn't aware of it, but I drifted ahead of Tyrone and the others. I moved toward Lou in a state of disbelief.

I heard Gordy say, "I guess Minnow burned the enchanter's head." His voice sounded a million miles away.

Lou's name came out of my mouth in the form of a question.

She replied by saying my name in the same questioning way.

A second of uncertainty passed before I ran to her. I told myself that when I reached her we would never be apart again.

The End of Book Six

Made in the USA
Middletown, DE
18 July 2015